A Million Views

To the kids who dream big and the friends who encourage them to dream even bigger—AS

PENGUIN WORKSHOP
An imprint of Penguin Random House LLC, New York

First published in the United States of America by Penguin Workshop,
an imprint of Penguin Random House LLC, New York, 2022

Text copyright © 2022 by Aaron Starmer
Jacket art copyright © 2022 by Penguin Random House LLC

Visit us online at penguinrandomhouse.com.

Library of Congress Cataloging-in-Publication Data is available.

Printed in the United States of America

ISBN 9780593386934

10 9 8 7 6 5 4 3 2 1 CJKB

Design by Sophie Erb

A Million Views

by

Aaron Starmer

Penguin Workshop

Chapter 1

The Problem with Bottomless Pits

Brewster Gaines had to push a friend into a bottomless pit. Simple enough, right? All he needed was the pit and the friend to push in. Plus some special effects to add in post.

Post, in case you don't know, is what directors call postproduction. And that's what Brewster was: a director. He made movies. Or to be completely accurate, he made videos. The latest video he was working on was called "What Do You Do with Friends Who Don't Return Your Messages?"

The answer to that age-old question? Push them into a bottomless pit, of course.

The whole thing was going to be about ten seconds long. The first five seconds would feature a boy, played by Brewster, holding a phone and approaching his friend while saying, "Hey, I messaged you two days ago! Why didn't you answer?" Then the friend would shrug, and the boy would run over and push the friend into the pit.

The other five seconds of the video would show the friend falling through the darkness of the pit, screaming, "I deserve thisssss!" while their body would get smaller and smaller but never hit anything.

Okay, maybe it wasn't that simple. In fact, Brewster discovered it was nearly impossible.

First, digging a bottomless pit was no easy task, even one that wasn't technically bottomless. Brewster only needed to dig one that *looked* bottomless from a certain angle, with specific lighting. It still took him hours to carve out anything even halfway suitable. He was a director, after all, not a backhoe.

Second, finding a friend to push into a bottomless pit was a little bit easier, though not much. Brewster had to convince someone to fall over backward multiple times. Because this video would require multiple takes. Twenty, at least. Maybe as many as fifty. The fall needed to be perfect, with the perfect windmilling arms and the perfect panicked facial expression. Anything less than perfect would mean the video would have no chance of going viral.

Finally, there was post—the aforementioned postproduction. That's all the editing and manipulating that Brewster had to do to the video once he completed the principal photography. In other words, after digging a suitable bottomless pit and finding a talented actor willing to be pushed into it over and over again, Brewster needed to create the special effect of having that actor's body continue to fall for a full five seconds. This would probably be quick work for someone who had professional 3D-rendering apps and skills with computer graphics, but Brewster had none of those things. He had access to the software that came with his six-year-old MacBook, and he had a willingness to try. In case you didn't know, old software and a willingness to try don't always translate into awe-inspiring special effects.

And so, Brewster was faced with a lot of problems to solve in order to create a ten-second video.

Which was fine. Which was great, actually. This was what he loved.

● ● ●

"It's ready," Brewster told Carly Lee on Thursday as they rode the bus to school.

He was talking about the pit. He'd spent the last three evenings digging, and it was finally the proper depth where it could pass as bottomless, so long as his phone was mounted correctly on the tripod and the sun wasn't too high in the sky.

Carly had agreed to play the role of the friend. She was a skateboarder and accustomed to falling. In fact, she was quite good at it.

"What time do you want to start?" she asked.

"As soon as school is over," he said. "Maybe sooner. Would you be willing to skip?"

"Would you be willing to dress up as me and take my detention?"

"I would," Brewster replied.

This wasn't a lie. Brewster had proven he was willing to suffer for his art. He'd broken bones—two fingers during a GoPro recording of a go-kart stunt at a local carnival. He'd contracted a stomach virus—after which he decided that working with toddlers, even well-behaved ones, might not be worth it. He'd been kicked out of Target more than once—store managers aren't always appreciative of stop-motion video productions being filmed in the produce section with borrowed toys. So yes, he was always ready to make some sacrifices to ensure top-notch productions.

At this point Carly was, shall we say, *less* dedicated, but she was still on board. "We'll take the bus home at the normal time," she said. "I'll get off at your stop and we'll start right away. But you better have snacks."

"Will potato chips work?" Brewster asked.

"What type?"

"Salt and . . ."

"Vinegar?"

Brewster nodded reluctantly. Salt and vinegar chips were an acquired taste, and one that not many people acquired.

"Acceptable," Carly finally said, and Brewster felt the relief wash over him. He also took a couple of mental notes: *In the future, buy a larger variety of snacks. For now, be thankful that Carly is very cool.*

Other than being very cool, Carly was a bit of a mystery. Brewster knew that she was a transplant from New Jersey and had moved into town at the beginning of the year. She seemed to be okay with living in Vermont, though sometimes she'd crack jokes about distinctly Vermont things, such as creemees and witch windows. He rode the bus with her, and they'd make small talk from time to time. She wasn't exactly his friend, but she tolerated him. Which was saying something, because not everyone tolerated Brewster.

Brewster would often see Carly at the skate park next to the playground where he filmed a lot of his videos. She was often filming videos too, skateboarding tricks that she'd post on her TikTok channel. She'd usually acknowledge his presence with a nod as she stood at the top of the quarter-pipe. Then she'd hop on her board and do something that was liable to break her neck. But she wouldn't break her neck because she, in her own words, "didn't completely suck."

When Brewster had approached her at that skate park a few days earlier and asked her to appear in "What Do You Do with Friends Who Don't Return Your Messages?" he did so saddled with low expectations. Since she wasn't exactly his friend, he didn't have to take her rejection personally. And he expected rejection. It came with the territory for visionaries like Brewster. Anything more would be considered an enormous win.

When her response was, "Sure, why not?" Brewster raised both hands in celebration. Which made Carly laugh. Her laugh was like chocolate milk. Really good.

Chapter 2

Character Motivation

Carly Lee chomped on salt and vinegar potato chips as Brewster set up the tripod.

"All I have to do is stand here and then you'll push me?" she asked.

"There's more to it than that," Brewster said. "When I walk up to your character, you've got to be ambivalent."

"Ambivalent?"

"It means you don't care."

"Got it."

"So think about something you don't care about."

"That's a lot of things."

"Focus on one."

"Okay. I'll think about owls."

Brewster paused to consider owls for a moment. Then he

asked, "What's wrong with owls?"

"They're creepy," she replied. "Not a fan."

"So you do care about owls, then?"

"What?"

"You're not ambivalent about owls," Brewster said. "Owls give you emotions. I need you to be emotionless. Think about something you don't care about at all. Something that gives you no feelings whatsoever."

"Fine." Carly closed her eyes. "Mustard. I'll think about mustard."

If it worked for her, then it worked for Brewster. He went back to setting up the tripod. He figured that the sun would be in the right position for at least forty-five minutes. The pit would look sufficiently black while the grass around it would look sufficiently green. That is, if he got the angle right. The stiff tripod wasn't doing him any favors.

"Here's an idea," Carly said. "What if I think about owls when you push me?"

Brewster opened a level app to make sure the phone was perfectly straight on the tripod before he answered. "What do you mean?"

Carly walked over to the pit, stood at its edge, and said, "So I'll be over here thinking about mustard, all like, 'Eh, mustard, who cares about mustard?' But then when you push me, I can be all like, 'Owls! Creepy owls everywhere! Owls, owls, owls!'"

She threw her arms in the air and waved them wildly. It was all a bit much, but Brewster couldn't tell her that. It was never a good idea to critique an actor so early in a shoot.

"We can definitely try that," Brewster said.

Directors in the not-too-distant past had to shoot on film, and while Brewster did have romantic notions about shooting on film, he knew that shooting on digital was the better choice for him. Film costs money because film is an actual thing. With digital, he could shoot for days and not worry. It took up hardly any space at all. It cost nothing. Or almost nothing—he had rented a terabyte of storage from Google for one year. Which meant he could humor his performers and do multiple takes without worrying about financial consequences.

"Let's do it, then," Carly said, and she practiced her flailing as Brewster stepped back from the tripod.

The framing was as good as it was going to get. It was time to shoot.

"Okay," Brewster said and tapped the circular red record icon. "We're rolling, but I'll say 'action' when it's time to do it. And let's do it over and over without stopping so we can make the best use of the current conditions."

"But I'll get dirty each time," Carly said. "Won't we have to, like, clean my clothes and comb my hair after each take?"

Good point. Why didn't Brewster think of that earlier? Because there were so many other things to consider, that's why.

Sound. Performance. The movement of the earth in relation to the sun!

"Okay," Brewster said. "We can't clean you up after every take, so we'll work with it. Let's pretend your character is an ambivalent . . . slob."

"Who hates owls," Carly added.

"Sure," Brewster said. "An owl-hating slob who's often ambivalent."

Carly nodded. "I'm okay with that."

"Does that mean you're ready?"

"As I'll ever be."

Good enough for Brewster, so he stepped out of frame and pointed to the spot where Carly was supposed to stand. He had marked it with a small black stone. Carly moved into position, and Brewster said, "Aaaand . . . action."

He counted quietly to three, then he paced into the frame while delivering his line: "Hey, I messaged you two days ago! Why didn't you answer?"

Carly shrugged her ambivalence. And he gave her a mighty push into the pit.

"Whoa," she said as she climbed out. "You really went for it there."

"I'm sorry," he said. "Did I hurt you?"

"No, no, no. I can handle it, but remember I'm a human person with bones and guts and everything."

"As long as you remember that this is art. And art is more important than people."

Whoops. Brewster immediately regretted saying that. This was why some people didn't tolerate him. Brewster's passion was overwhelming. Feelings were always secondary. Or tertiary, which meant they came third. Or maybe even farther down the list. His videos—his art!—would always be number one, and he could never imagine anything else muscling its way into the top slot.

Again, he was lucky that Carly was very cool. She snorted. "You're a funny kid, Brewster. Just promise not to break my arm, okay?"

"Technically, I can't make that promise," Brewster said, because he was an honest guy, and injuries can never be entirely ruled out on a set.

Carly shrugged and replied, "Fine. Promise me if you do break my arm, it will at least look amazing."

"That I can do," Brewster said.

He took one more mental note: *In the future, make all actors sign a contract that says if they break their arms, then they can't sue me.*

● ● ●

They did it over and over, twenty times at least, and Brewster let his phone continue recording throughout. Carly got quite good at her part, improving her reactions with every take, and always displaying her natural charisma and athleticism. The only reason they had to stop the filming was because of Brewster's neighbor from across the street, Piper Barnes.

"Brewster Gaines!" Piper hollered as she strode across the yard pointing at him. "What the heck do you think you're doing?"

Before Brewster could respond, Piper shouldered him out of the way and came to Carly's aid. "Are you okay?" she asked.

"Why wouldn't I be?" Carly responded.

"Because this little psycho was pushing you into a hole." Piper glared at Brewster as she said it.

Carly laughed.

"What's so funny?" Piper said.

"You called Brewster a psycho," Carly said. "Li'l harmless Brewster."

Brewster didn't like being called a psycho. Or li'l. Or harmless. And he certainly didn't like Piper interrupting his production. "We're wasting valuable time," he said. "We can only shoot for another ten minutes. No distractions."

"Wait," Piper whispered to Carly. "You're okay with this?"

Carly shrugged. "He's not paying me or anything, but it's still kinda fun. I'm curious how it'll turn out. And what people will think of it."

Piper looked at Carly, then at the hole, then at Brewster, then at the phone mounted on the tripod, then back at Carly, then back at the hole, then back at Brewster.

"I don't care if it's fun or whatever it is," Piper said to Brewster, and she started walking away. "You don't go around pushing girls!"

Piper was in high school—a freshman—and Brewster and Carly were in sixth grade. That meant that Piper was wiser and more mature. At least that's what it was supposed to mean. To Brewster, it seemed like Piper's three extra years of life had sucked the joy out of her.

Piper was filled with joy when she was their age. Brewster remembered. She used to dance in her yard when the dandelions were thick, twirling her arms and humming Taylor Swift songs. She used to lie in her hammock and read graphic novels that would make her giggle. But that was a few years ago. An eternity. These days Piper was withdrawn and often annoyed, if not angry, with the world. Deep down, Brewster knew this wasn't his fault, but that didn't mean he didn't sometimes think that it was.

As Piper crossed the street and headed back toward her home, Brewster apologized to Carly. "That's Piper," he said. "She's grumpy."

"Just a girl looking out for another girl," Carly said. "Nothing wrong with that."

"I guess not."

"You know what?" Carly said. "We've done enough takes. I

should go. I promised to help Mom and Ken with dinner."

Great, Brewster thought, *Piper ruined the rhythm of the shoot, and now Carly is bored.* "Ten more takes, that's all I need," Brewster said. "To make sure it's perfect. And then we have to do the green screen work."

"Green screen?" she said. "You never said anything about a green screen."

"Sure I did," Brewster said, because he was sure that he did. He had dyed a white sheet neon green specifically for the occasion.

"I don't know what a green screen is, but we can green screen some other time," Carly said as she picked up her backpack, which she'd stashed behind a tree.

"But we need to finish it tonight!" Brewster yelped.

"What's the rush?"

"It's already Thursday. I've gotta post by Friday night. That way it has two days to build steam and go semi-viral by Sunday night, and then on Monday morning, when people are goofing off at school or work because they wish it was still the weekend, they'll share it over and over, and by the end of the week it'll be on late-night TV and local news and . . . everywhere."

Carly stared at Brewster for a second, then shrugged. "Seems likely. Doesn't change the fact that I've gotta help Mom and Ken with dinner. I'm all in for international fame, but it will have to wait a few more days."

Chapter 3

Instructions for Loneliness

Brewster went inside. He didn't need to help with dinner because no one in his family helped with dinner. His mom always picked something up on her way home from work. Mondays and Wednesdays were burritos or Chinese. Tuesdays and Thursdays were Subway days. Fridays were pizza. On the weekends, they'd sometimes go out to eat, depending on who was around, and sometimes they'd fend for themselves.

Brewster's parents sometimes traveled a lot for work—his father specialized in training for a software company, and his mother was a marketer for an environmental nonprofit. They had moved to Vermont from Boston when Brewster was barely walking. They were in search of a slower pace, and in some ways, they found it, but only when they were home.

Brewster had an older sibling named Jade. Jade was nonbinary, and their pronouns were *they* and *them*. They were seventeen and had an active life filled with friends and school and employment. Whenever they were around, they'd stay up watching horror movies, and the house was often filled with shrieks and howls late into the night. It didn't bother Brewster. He realized that Jade wouldn't be living with them for much longer once they went to college, so it was comforting to know that his sibling was right down the hall, doing what made them happy.

But there was no getting around the truth. Their family simply didn't spend much time together. When the nightly dinner arrived, usually half of it would be placed straight in the fridge and then whoever was home would take their portions to eat in front of a screen of some sort.

It hadn't always been like that. There used to be family dinners. There was even some home cooking every now and again. But as the parents got busier—with work and private interests—so too did the kids. They all slipped into their own spaces until that became so routine that having an actual dinner as an entire family seemed monumentally weird.

Tonight was no different from any other night. Brewster's mom sent him a cheery text:

> I'll be down the street at Lisa's if you need me. Celebrating her new job! Your favorite sandwich is on the kitchen counter.

As Brewster ate his Italian B.M.T. with olives and sweet peppers, he sat on his bed with his MacBook and went over the day's footage. There were some good takes in the mix. But the ones with his best performance weren't the ones with Carly's best performance. He wished he could overlay different takes to create one fluid one, but he didn't know how. Using an outdated version of iMovie, he could trim clips, insert transitions, add audio, and apply filters, but not much more than that. The app was best suited for editing videos of weddings and family reunions, not for creating viral sensations.

Though perhaps he was overthinking things. More than half the videos that went viral weren't planned at all. They were random moments. Some stupid, some sublime, all magical in their own way. It was a magic that Brewster often chased, which meant pulling out his phone whenever life offered up an interesting moment. Some people might've accused Brewster of hiding behind a screen. What he was actually doing was grabbing at remarkable chunks of existence with the hopes of sharing them with the world. Easier said than done.

As for other viral videos, they were either cranked out by stunningly attractive people who danced or lip-synched while being attractive, or they were crafted by pros, people who could perform or who were adept at video manipulation. These masters could rattle off funny voices and facts and facial expressions. They could create amazing animations or perhaps re-edit trailers for horror movies and make them seem like comedies. They could film perfect spoof songs or skits skewering the latest pop culture or news events. Their talents, and their skill sets, seemed endless.

All that Brewster had to work with were the multiple takes of a kid pushing another kid. As he watched it—alone in his room, his half-eaten sandwich on the bed next to him—he started to see it as Piper must have seen it. As violent. As mean. As a boy pushing a girl into a hole. And there was nothing funny about that.

Maybe it would work better once he filmed Carly from above as she lay on the green sheet with her arms and legs flailing. He did at least know how to swap out green for black in iMovie to make it look like she was falling into the darkness, but he still had to figure out how to make her body get smaller and smaller for the effect to work. It would definitely improve the joke, especially with her screaming, "I deserve thisssss!"

Or maybe it would make it even worse. Was it funny for a victim to say they deserved an awful fate? He thought it could be. The joke was that no one likes being ignored, and so to get revenge on the person ignoring you was bound to make an audience smile. But was Carly the best villain?

Of course she wasn't. He was.

Carly had only lived in town since the fall, but she was already more popular than Brewster, who had lived here since he was a baby. That said something to him about likability. The villain should never be more likable than the hero. More entertaining, perhaps, but never more likable, a cardinal rule of storytelling.

It was settled, then. Brewster closed his laptop and fetched the green sheet from his closet. He could film the falling segment now, by himself, and then invite Carly over tomorrow to refilm the pushing segment, but with *her* pushing *him*.

He spread the sheet flat on the floor, then placed a long pillow in the center of it, so that he could lie on something comfortable and minimize wrinkling in the sheet. Then he grabbed his tripod and positioned and adjusted it so that he could mount his phone directly above and achieve the overhead view.

For lighting, he needed bright but not harsh, and he found the best combination was to use the overhead light and a lamp with a white sheet draped over it. When everything was as he wanted it, he started recording. Then he got flat on his back on the pillow and screamed, "I deserve thisssss!" while wiggling like a newborn.

He did it five times before there was a knock on the door.

"Yikes. Do I wanna know?" his dad asked as he stepped into the room.

Brewster rolled over. "This looks weird. I get it."

Spotting the tripod and phone, his dad said, "Another video? Which I'm guessing explains that hole you've been digging outside?"

"Yeah. I'll show you when I'm done."

Brewster's dad encouraged his videos. Or to be more accurate, he didn't discourage them. He enjoyed watching them, or at least pretended to, though he was never an active participant. Whenever Brewster asked him to be involved, he said things like, "You don't want this ugly mug on-screen. It'll scare the children."

When he was in elementary school, Brewster had visions of his family becoming online sensations, the type where the mom and dad sing funny songs about Christmas shopping or Little League or minivans, while the kids dance and make silly faces in the background. Of course, his family never was and never would be like this, so Brewster had to pursue his dream as a solo artist.

"How's your sandwich?" his dad asked as Brewster flattened the wrinkles out of the green sheet.

"Sandwichy," Brewster said.

"I wanted to let you know I'm staying at the airport hotel tonight," his dad said. "Early flight in the morning."

"When will you be back?"

"Not sure. A week or so?"

Not a short business trip, but certainly not his dad's longest. "Where are you going?"

"Portland. Oregon, not Maine."

"When the video goes live, I'll check the analytics and see if it hits bigger out there than here."

Some of Brewster's previous videos weren't complete failures. A few even achieved over one thousand views. According to YouTube analytics, an odd ten-second bit titled "A Duck Orders Breakfast" was viewed at least five hundred times in the Cleveland, Ohio, metropolitan area alone. Brewster couldn't explain it. Sometimes things are popular in one place but not another.

Still, hundreds or thousands of views were peanuts compared to what truly made a difference. At a certain point, Brewster had decided there was a magic number of views, a benchmark he had to reach if he were ever to make a true impact.

A million.

Whenever Brewster saw a seven-digit number below a video, he paid attention. Because he knew that other people were paying attention. Other people were sharing. Other people were saying, "Look at this, because *this* is worthwhile." Brewster knew that he was good at what he did, and that he was getting better every day. He didn't, however, know if his videos were worthwhile.

They were to him, of course. But were they worthwhile to others? To his family? To his schoolmates? To the world? And, if so, what did that say about Brewster? A million views could tell him that. In the meantime, he had to keep working, to keep cranking out videos until one of them broke through the noise of YouTube.

"Looks like you have some special effects in this one," his dad said, cocking his chin at the green sheet.

"Bottomless pit," Brewster explained.

His dad's eyes narrowed, and he nodded slightly. "Practical effects still beat out CGI any day. At least in my book."

Brewster nodded. "A combo of both. That's the key."

"You're the expert," his dad said, and then he grabbed Brewster around the shoulders, pulled him in close, and kissed him on the top of the head where his hair parted. "Be good," his dad told him, before heading out the door.

There was no "I love you" or "I'll miss you" or "I'll bring you something back," like other kids probably heard when their dads left. But that was fine. This was normal for Brewster. Expected.

It was also expected that he would stay up too late, tinkering with iMovie, figuring out how to make this all work. Maybe he'd even fall asleep on the floor, under the green sheet, without anyone else popping in to check on him.

In fact, that's exactly what happened.

Chapter 4

A Portal Story

Brewster yawned as he sat on a swing. Most sixth-graders felt they were too old or too cool for the swings, so that's where Brewster sat during recess when he wanted to be alone. Which was often.

It didn't always work. Like today, for instance, when Liam Wentworth approached him. Liam was a perfectly nice kid. Probably too nice. He was the type of guy you didn't want to invite to your birthday party because he'd be hovering around you at every moment—cake cutting, present opening, you get the picture. But, for the same reason, you felt bad not inviting him. He lived for those events. Cherished them. And yet he was needy. Clingy. Loyal to a fault. That's why whenever he tried to talk to Brewster, Brewster always tried to nip the conversation in the bud.

So, when Liam asked, "Is this swing taken?" Brewster responded, "Yes, by her."

His arm shot up and he pointed across the playground to Carly. He might as well have been pointing to a grizzly bear, because the sight of a girl with confidence and swagger sapped this kindly boy of any of both he might've had.

"Okay, sorry, but I want you to know that I subscribed to your channel and I'm looking forward to your next video," Liam told him, before scurrying away.

Brewster was already aware that Liam had subscribed because he checked his subscriber numbers every morning. His channel currently had 43 subscribers, which wasn't many, but also wasn't nothing. When that number went up or down, it usually dictated Brewster's mood for the day. Liam's subscription had brought him from 42 to 43, but it didn't move him much, because Brewster knew that Liam was a fan of everything and everyone. Still, his videos needed as many eyes as they could get, so he wasn't going to complain.

Speaking of eyes, Carly's were now focused on Brewster. Pointing at her had seemed to summon her, because within a few moments, she was at the swings. And there was another girl with her. Carly started to make an introduction. "Brewster, you might already know—"

"Hey, Rosa," Brewster said with a sigh. "Are you here for your five dollars?"

Rosa Blake was chewing on a thumbnail and watching Brewster carefully. She was a tall girl, with high shoulders and a sharp chin that made her seem much older than her peers. She was also a quiet girl, but a certain kind of quiet. Not shy, exactly. She simply didn't talk unless she had something to say. That meant she stared at people a lot, and in a way that made Brewster think she was reading their thoughts. Which was a bit impressive, and more than a bit creepy.

Six months earlier, during a field trip to a science museum, Rosa had loaned Brewster five dollars. Brewster was trying to purchase a water rocket, but didn't have enough money, so he was asking the cashier to "cut me a deal." It was holding up the line, and Rosa just wanted to buy Twizzlers, so she slapped a five-dollar bill on the counter and told Brewster to "take the spaceship and move along."

He had yet to pay her back.

"I don't need money," Rosa told Brewster at the swings. "I'm here for Carly."

"She's my agent," Carly said.

Rosa shook her head.

"Okay," Carly went on, "she's not exactly my agent, but she's smart, and I told her about the video, and we both have some thoughts on my part and how to make it better."

Rosa nodded.

"Sorry, but your part has already been rewritten," Brewster

said. "I'm now the one who falls into the hole, and you're the one who does the pushing."

Carly flinched. "What? You? No. No. I'm in the hole. Me. That's the better part."

"Actually," Brewster said, and he kicked off from the ground and started swinging, "it isn't your call. I'm the writer and director, so it's my call. And my call is that I'm in the hole."

For a few seconds, Carly just stood there glaring at him. Then she opened her mouth but didn't say anything. Finally, she stomped away.

Rosa remained in place. She stared at Brewster as he continued to swing, his legs pumping with force so he could get higher and thus farther away from her.

"I don't have the five dollars," he told her.

"And I told you I don't care," Rosa responded. "Money is not important to me."

Every once in a while, a very fancy car that was very low to the ground and very red and very loud would drop Rosa off at school. Apparently, it was an Italian car, which made it especially fancy. So Brewster knew that Rosa's parents were wealthy. But she, herself, never drew attention to that fact. She was the opposite of a show-off. She didn't flaunt designer clothes or expensive toys or gadgets. She ate tuna fish sandwiches and apples for every lunch. If you didn't focus on her height and her piercing stare, she was easy to ignore.

"If you don't want the money, then why are you still here?" Brewster asked her.

"Like I told you, for Carly," Rosa said.

"Carly is still in the video. But since she's more likable than I am, she's now the protagonist. That's a win for her. She doesn't have to fall anymore."

Rosa shook her head. "Not enough. You're gonna expand her role. Make this a portal story."

"A what?"

"You know. *Stranger Things*? Narnia? A portal opens. A girl goes through. Ends up in a magical world. Your hole is the portal. That's the story."

Brewster's feet hit the ground hard, then skidded through the gravel directly below the swing until he came to a stop. "This is a ten-second YouTube video."

"YouTube?"

"Yeah. So? That's where I post."

"Why not TikTok? Snapchat? Or—"

"Or what about Vine?"

"What's Vine?"

"Exactly. You don't know it because it's not around anymore. YouTube isn't going anywhere," Brewster said, which was something he said to anyone who questioned his choice of platforms. "Other sites? Here today, gone tomorrow. YouTube is forever."

"Forever?" Rosa said. "Unlikely. It *does* have the biggest audience, though. I'll give you that. But ten seconds is too short for YouTube."

She wasn't wrong. The most popular YouTube videos tended to be in the two-to-five-minute range. If anyone knew this, it was Brewster. Problem was, he never had enough resources, material, or actors to create videos that long.

"I'm not changing anything," he told her. "I've got a plan, and I'm sticking to it."

Rosa nodded and chewed at her thumbnail for a few moments, before announcing, "We'll be at your house after school."

Then she pivoted on her heel and strode away from the swings.

Brewster could've yelled something. He could've chased after her. He could've told her to go home and watch his videos and then she'd understand why he needed to be in charge of everything. Instead, he simply watched her long, confident stride as she disappeared behind the structures.

Chapter 5

A Trailer for a Movie That Doesn't Exist

Carly and Rosa sat together in the first seat of the bus, so when they got off at Brewster's house, they were in front of him. He couldn't stop the girls as they rushed to the hole, and by the time he joined them, they were already discussing things.

"It should be like a flash," Carly said, arms in the air. "Light everywhere. And a sound like *zzzzzoooop!*"

"No," Rosa said, the toe of her sneaker tracing the edge of the hole. "Silence and darkness. Like being swallowed up by oil."

Brewster cleared his throat to get their attention, and when he had it, he pointed at Rosa and said, "You weren't invited."

"Sure she was," Carly said. "I invited her."

"But you're not even friends," Brewster said.

"How do you know that?" Carly replied.

"I never see the two of you having lunch together, or even

talking much," Brewster said.

"Have you really watched us that closely?" Carly asked.

The answer was no. But Brewster liked people to believe that he was an observant person—he was an artist, after all, and artists are prized for their skills of observation. So he wasn't about to admit that he didn't actually know anything about the friendship between these two girls.

"Fine, your BFF can watch us film," he said. "But I never asked for any ideas. I don't want them. I don't need them."

"What about my money?" Rosa said plainly.

"Your . . . ?"

Carly stepped forward and put a hand on Brewster's shoulder. "Here's the deal, lemon peel."

"Lemon peel?" Brewster asked.

"It's a saying," Carly said.

Brewster looked to Rosa for confirmation, and Rosa shrugged.

"I have never heard anyone say that," Brewster replied.

"Well then, Brew Dog, you should get out more," Carly said. "What we're trying to tell you is that Rosa has signed on as the producer. And I'll be the star. You'll be the director. Have you ever seen a trailer?"

"Like for a movie? Of course."

"Okay. So that's what we're making now, a trailer." Carly said, and her face brightened. "For a blockbuster movie called

Carly Lee and the Land of Shadows."

"It's a working title," Rosa added.

Brewster gently pushed Carly's hand off his shoulder, then he walked over to the hole, climbed inside, and lay down on his back.

"What? The? Heck?" Carly said.

"Bury me," Brewster said gravely. "I'm not needed anymore. You've got it all figured out."

The girls leaned over the edge of the hole for a better look. Brewster imagined that this was what it must be like to be awake at your own funeral. That is, if you were being buried without a coffin.

Carly shook her head. "You're weird."

But Rosa sprouted a rare smile. "You heard him." Then she kicked a clod of dirt down onto Brewster's chest.

"Hey!" Brewster shouted as he sat straight up. "That was uncalled-for."

"That's exactly what you called for," Rosa said. "And I understand. You don't want my money."

This wasn't true. Brewster wanted any money he could get. He only had about ten dollars to his name, which was all that remained from the fifty dollars his grandma gave him for his twelfth birthday. He had no allowance to rely on, and his parents never had much to spare for his productions. His videos weren't underfunded. They were *unfunded.*

"So what?" Brewster said. "You give me ten dollars to buy my time? Directors get paid a lot more than that. Especially if it's a work for hire."

"I'm not paying you," Rosa said. "But you can have a percentage when we sell the actual rights to the movie. I'll make you a coproducer."

"Oh, so now I work for free, and you spend ten dollars on what? Lunch for you and Carly or something?"

"Why do you keep saying ten dollars?" Rosa asked.

"Yeah," Carly said. "She's got a lot more than that."

"Okay, then," Brewster said. "Twenty dollars."

"Try five thousand," Rosa said plainly.

Brewster was still sitting in the hole. He wasn't sure if he should lie back down or jump right up. This number was . . . well . . .

"You didn't say five thousand?"

"She sure did," Carly replied, eyebrows going up and down.

"That's only for the trailer," Rosa said. "The budget for the actual movie will be *a lot* more. Millions. Maybe Disney will invest."

"Right now, you . . . you . . . you have five thousand dollars?" Brewster asked.

Rosa nodded.

"To spend on a trailer?"

She nodded again.

"For a movie that doesn't even exist?"

She nodded once more.

This was an unfathomable amount of money to Brewster. Simply impossible.

"You two should go home," he said, climbing out of the hole. "I can't deal with this right now."

An understatement. He could barely stand. He felt dizzy, queasy, entirely out of sorts. Some things were too good to be true, and this was one of those things. Because people with lots of money don't offer it to filmmakers. It was always the other way around. Filmmakers had to go in search of financing for their movies, which was notoriously tricky. Brewster had even heard about a director who couldn't get anyone to fund his project, so in a last-ditch effort, he went to churches and begged for money to make a religious film. Then he used that money to make a horror movie instead.

In Brewster's situation, he was the one being tricked. Obviously these girls were setting him up for a prank. There was no other explanation. But he wasn't about to fall for it.

"I'm going inside," he told them, and he headed for the door.

Carly called out to him, "We'll be figuring out a script until you get back. Bring snacks. Chiiiiips!"

As soon as Brewster was inside, he headed to the kitchen, where he opened the fridge and pulled out a big jug of chocolate milk. He poured it into one of the pint glasses his mom typically drank beer out of, and he chugged it down as he watched the girls through the window.

They paced around the hole and crouched next to it. They pointed. They talked. They didn't appear to be joking around or pretending for Brewster's benefit. They honestly looked like they were planning something.

"Hey, bro," a voice said from behind him.

Brewster turned around to find Jade at the fridge, grabbing a Diet Coke.

"Hey," Brewster said.

"New friends?" Jade asked, cocking their chin toward the window.

"I don't know," Brewster said. "Coworkers maybe."

This made Jade laugh, perhaps because Jade knew their twelve-year-old brother didn't have the slightest idea what it was like to deal with actual coworkers. Brewster, obviously, had never been employed. Jade, on the other hand, had a job. A real job. They were a cashier at the grocery store and worked more hours than they probably should've, considering they had senior year of high school to finish.

They seemed constantly exhausted. More often than not, Brewster would find Jade asleep on the couch, while some scary movie streamed on the TV. It would always remind Brewster of the days when the two of them would stay up late watching movies together, a passion passed down from their dad. But like their dad, Jade never had much interest in filming anything with Brewster. It was easy to blame the age gap, the older sibling embarrassed to be at the whim of the younger one. Clearly Jade was also too busy. They had been for the last few years.

That didn't mean that Jade didn't care about their younger brother, though. During the occasional moments when Brewster saw them awake, they would dispense bits of advice that fell somewhere between wisdom and riddles. Like on that afternoon in the kitchen.

"I don't know who those two girls are to you," Jade told Brewster. "But please don't get embroiled in some sort of love triangle, okay?"

"What? No. That's—"

"I'm just telling you that our family doesn't need any extra drama right now," Jade said as they cracked their soda and headed toward their room. "It's on you to keep being a goofy little kid. Forget this mess."

Mess? What mess? The only mess Brewster was aware of was the mess the world seemed to be making of his plans.

Jade was gone before Brewster could ask what they meant. And when he checked the window again, the girls were gone too.

Chapter 6

Winner Winner Chicken Dinner

That night, Brewster dreamt. Usually he would forget his dreams, but whenever he woke in the morning, he'd have a vague feeling about whether they'd been good dreams or nightmares. He always preferred waking from the nightmares. That probably seems odd, but to Brewster it was like the feeling he had when he was getting over an illness. Clear head, still stomach, back to normal. What was better than that? To Brewster, not much. Unfortunately, that night Brewster dreamt a very good dream. And unfortunately, he remembered it all.

There wasn't much to the dream. It started quite realistically. Brewster was in bed, laptop in front of him, reviewing his YouTube videos, like he did dozens of times every week. But this is where things started to turn. He was looking at the video for "What Do You Do with Friends Who Don't Return Your

Messages?" He hadn't even finished, let alone uploaded, that video in real life, but here in the dream world it was complete and available for public viewing. Admittedly, that wasn't too strange. This was a dream, after all.

It also wasn't strange that a number appeared below the left-hand corner of the video, displaying the video's views. The count currently stood at 1,111. A symmetrical, but still relatively small number. In real life, if Brewster hit refresh on his browser, he might be lucky enough to see the views on a video like this climb by one, to watch as 1,111 became 1,112. Which was always nice.

But in this dream, something more than nice happened. Something miraculous occurred. Even without refreshing the browser, the number began to climb up and up and up.

5,000 . . . 10,000 . . . 50,000 . . . 100,000!

Faster and faster, the numbers rolling over, virality taking hold in real time. And not only that. There was sound that went along with it, bells and chimes that Brewster associated with casinos. He had accompanied his parents to Las Vegas a few years ago when his father was working at a trade show. They stayed in a hotel that was shaped like a pyramid, and when they walked through the lobby, it was an explosion of bright colors and happy noises. Brewster wasn't old enough to gamble, but he instantly understood why people did. The thrill of winning paired with such intoxicating sounds!

250,000 . . . 500,000!

The number of views was racing toward a million, and though he didn't want to look up from the screen, he was compelled to because the sound seamlessly morphed from mechanized melodies to recognizable voices. His family's voices. They were instantly in the room with him. His mom, dad, and Jade, crouching at the foot of Brewster's bed, pumping their fists and chanting.

"Winner winner chicken dinner! Winner winner chicken dinner!"

It was something kids said at recess sometimes, but never about Brewster, because Brewster rarely participated in, let alone won, the games they played. Still, it felt fantastic to hear his family saying it and to see them proud and smiling, and when he finally looked back down at the laptop to see how many views the video had gotten, the number was—

He didn't know. Because the dream was over. He had woken up. Alone in his room. His laptop on the bed next to him. Back to his drab reality.

The dream had stirred such amazing feelings in him, but he wasn't sure which part was more exciting. Watching the views tick up? Or listening to his proud family? Since he wanted to keep the vibe going, the first thing Brewster did after he woke up was check his YouTube videos. He needed to see if, by some miracle, the dream had been a premonition. Maybe his views had shot into the stratosphere.

No luck. The only difference was that there was now a new comment below one video, a stop-motion oddity called "High Atop Mount Mashed Potato." The comment was, of course, from Liam Wentworth.

Close encounters of the yummy kind!

It was a weird thing to write, and Brewster didn't understand it. But he didn't want to be cruel, so he clicked the thumbs-up icon next to it. Not that anyone besides Liam would even notice. "High Atop Mount Mashed Potato" had stalled out at fewer than two hundred views. Perhaps half of those came from Liam.

Rather than dwell on that sad fact, Brewster closed the MacBook and turned to his phone. That's where he was confronted with another message. Only this time it was from Carly.

READ OUR SCRIPT!

And there was a PDF attached, a file called FINAL DRAFT. Brewster opened it immediately.

CARLY LEE AND THE LAND OF SHADOWS
A movie trailer from Rosa Blake Productions

It'll start like lots of movie trailers. You know kind of normal with Carly Lee waking up, going to school, skateboarding and other stuff but then she sees this hole and she's like what's this all about? She tries to jump or maybe ollie over it with her skateboard but falls inside and WHOA!

There's bunches of color or darkness or maybe some lightning bolts and then we see all these really fast glimpses of the Land of Shadows. It's a gray place where there are blob monsters and smoke ravens and a dark wizard. It'll feel epic and there will be music that's all violins and booming drums but we can't give away too much of the plot because that's always annoying and we haven't figured it all out anyway.

The trailer ends with a cliffhanger of some sort and a creepy whisper. "Don't get lost in the shadow." Then the title pops up followed by the words COMING SOON!

After everyone watches the trailer they'll be like, "Yes! I need to see that. When can I see it?" And we'll have to tell them that if they give us a ton of money we'll make the actual movie and it'll come out in the next year hopefully on Netflix. After that we can all quit school and become superstars.

Sound good?

We start this morning.

It was Saturday. Brewster usually spent Saturday mornings catching up on videos from his favorite YouTube channels. Sometimes he'd take notes about things that worked, and things that didn't work. If he'd taken notes on this "script," they would've been entirely about things that didn't work.

Brewster sighed and set his phone on his dresser, then grabbed a pair of rumpled jeans off the floor and pulled them on. A sliver of window between the curtains revealed a sight he most certainly did not want to see. The girls were in the backyard again, but this time they had been joined by Brewster's mom.

He double-timed it outside, not even bothering to put on shoes or flatten his stubborn cowlick. "This is getting out of hand," he grumbled as he approached. But nobody seemed to hear him. They were deep in conversation.

"So it's like *Alice in Wonderland*?" his mom asked.

"Considerably darker," Rosa explained. "Not all that kiddie stuff."

"We hate kiddie stuff, Jenny," Carly added.

Brewster's mom's name was Jennifer, but her friends all called her Jen. Or Jenny, if they were close friends. As far as Brewster knew, this was the first time Carly had met his mom. Not exactly a qualification for being at the Jenny level.

That said, Jenny didn't seem to mind. She smiled at Carly and told her, "When I was your age, my friends choreographed dance routines. New Kids on the Block, et cetera, et cetera. I thought we should dance to My Bloody Valentine instead."

Jenny laughed to herself, but the two girls didn't make a sound.

"In other words, not all that kiddie stuff," she went on.

Again, nothing. Clearly Carly and Rosa didn't have a clue about the differences between pop idols and indie bands of the early 1990s. Did that make Jenny the world's coolest mom, with dark and obscure tastes? Or the world's saddest mom, hopelessly out of touch with today's youth? Brewster didn't want her to be either. Therefore, he changed the subject.

"I'm not sure why everyone is so insistent on—" he started to say.

But Carly cut him off, zapping him with finger guns and asking, "Didja get the script?"

"I did," Brewster answered.

"And I'm guessing there are no moms in this script, so I'll take this as my cue to leave," Jenny said and then pushed her son on the shoulder and added, "Morning, lazybones, there are bagels for whoever wants them," before turning and heading toward the house.

The push wasn't violent. In fact, coming from his mom, it would've qualified as affectionate. But Brewster acted like it didn't happen. In fact, he tried not to move a muscle. This was his strategy for making it seem like he was in complete control. He ignored his mom, keeping his focus squarely on Carly. (He couldn't possibly focus on Rosa, because Rosa, of course, was staring at him, and probably judging him, for the bare feet, the cowlick, the mother who pushed her son instead of kissing him on the forehead.)

"Your script wasn't a script," Brewster told Carly.

"Well then, what was it? Because it wasn't a turkey sandwich," Carly said. "We think it's pretty amazing, actually. Can't you picture the movie on opening night?"

She held up two opposing Ls with her fingers, the universal gesture for a movie screen.

"I can't picture it *at all*," Brewster said. "Because you need the right format for a script if you want anyone to picture it."

In his peripheral vision, Brewster noticed that Rosa was still staring at him. But now she was nodding and saying, "Help us with the right format, then. You're the expert. That's your job. Make the ideas come to life."

It was the sort of comment that both charmed and stung. Rosa had called him an expert, and that felt good. But she had also strongly implied that *he* was working for *them*. Or, more likely, for *her*. She had the money, after all.

The money. So much money. Five thousand dollars. It would take decades of saving allowances for Brewster to have that much. And his parents had never even given him an allowance! Which meant he had to remind himself that turning down the chance to work on a project with such a large budget would be a colossal mistake. This whole thing was feeling less like a prank and more like an opportunity that might pass him by if he didn't play his cards right. So he gritted his teeth and accepted his position.

"Come inside," he told them.

Chapter 7

Proper Screenplay Format

                                                      FADE IN:

INT. BEDROOM—MORNING

Our trailer opens in a girl's bedroom. It's filled
with posters and stuffies and pink things.

CARLY LEE (12 and brave) is asleep in bed. Sun
shines through the window onto her face. She
wakes. She sits up.

                        CARLY
                    (groaning)
                Mondays . . .

"See," Brewster said, pointing to the words on his MacBook.
"That's how you do it. Slug line. Description. Action. Character.

Dialogue. All the essentials."

Carly and Rosa were sitting at his sides, and they were all sitting on his bed with his laptop in front of them. Jade had walked by a few moments earlier and snickered when they saw the trio, but Brewster swatted a hand at them, telling them to keep moving.

"Why all the . . . stuff?" Carly asked.

"What do you mean by stuff?" Brewster replied.

"Well, like, I think it's saying that I'm twelve years old and I'm brave," Carly said. "I already know I'm twelve and brave."

"Okay, but the director doesn't know that," Brewster told her.

"But the director is *you*," Carly responded. "You know that I'm twelve and brave because you wrote that I'm twelve and brave. And because I am those things in real life, and you know me in real life."

"She's got a point," Rosa said.

Brewster almost didn't want to respond. Months ago, he'd read a few books on rules of screenwriting. So he knew a thing or two about a thing or two. Did he need to explain how you properly introduce characters, or why you only use 12-point Courier font, or where exactly you set the margins for action and dialogue? Would he have to describe what slug lines were and how they showed whether settings were interior (INT) or exterior (EXT) while at the same time establishing shots and scenes? Was he expected to teach the well-defined rules of a one-hundred-year-old craft to people who obviously didn't care to follow them?

No. He had to put things simply.

"Do you want me to be the director?" Brewster asked the girls.

Carly hesitated. Then shrugged. Rosa nodded emphatically.

"Okay," he went on. "To be a good director, I need the script to be in proper screenplay format."

"That makes sense," Rosa said.

"You didn't have a proper format when we were doing the bottomless pit video," Carly told him. "You didn't even have a, you know, script or screenplay or whatever."

"Yeah," Brewster said. "Because the video was ten seconds long and had two shots. This trailer will be a few minutes, right?"

"Probably ten minutes," Carly said.

"No more than three," Rosa said firmly. "We need to keep it under three."

"And it has multiple shots and locations and effects and actors—"

Brewster stopped himself for a moment. Actors. Of course, actors! They had Carly Lee in the starring role, and she had the potential to be quite good in it, but he was beginning to realize they'd need at least a few other people to pull this thing off. And with every moment that passed, Brewster was discovering that he did want to pull this thing off.

Rosa, of course, was already a step ahead of him. That's why she said, "I can put together a list."

"A list of what?" Carly asked.

"Cast members," Rosa said. "And crew. We'll need people who are good with makeup and costumes and all that other stuff."

"How many people is that?" Carly asked.

"Brewster?" Rosa said.

His answer was an honest one. "I really don't know. I'm pretty sure that's what the producer figures out."

And there it was again: Rosa's stare, laser focused on Brewster's eyes. Was she angry? It seemed possible. Though the range of emotions Brewster had come to associate with Rosa didn't usually include anger; it mostly fluttered between mild disinterest and curious contempt.

When she finally spoke, Brewster was relieved, partly because of what she said, but mostly because he found that Rosa's voice was almost always preferable to her silence, particularly when she was staring at him.

"I can take care of it," she said with a firm nod.

"So, like, who else are we talking about?" Carly asked.

"We need a dark wizard, right?" Brewster said, remembering the character mentioned in their sad attempt at a script.

"Yep," Carly confirmed. "Someone who's evil to the core. A total villain."

"Or someone who can act evil," Rosa said. "In sixth grade, there's one person who comes to mind, right?"

Brewster knew exactly who she meant. An outcast and a snob. A pompous person, who puzzled most people. To put it plainly: the only kid who could out-Brewster Brewster.

"You're not—" he started to say.

But once again, Carly cut him off. "Oh my god. You mean Godfrey Tarkington."

Rosa nodded.

Brewster's only response was, "Please no."

Chapter 8

Battling Blobulor

There was an old tennis court, along a dirt road, within walking distance of Brewster's house. That's where they found Godfrey Tarkington. They weren't looking for him there. But as Brewster, Rosa, and Carly headed up the road toward where Godfrey lived, they couldn't possibly miss him.

He was dressed like a medieval knight, draped in light chain mail—hood, shirt, and gloves—and wielding a long knobbly stick. The tall metal fence around the tennis court was wrapped in vines, and there were weeds erupting from the cracks in the faded green pavement, which made it all look like a forested arena. And that's essentially what Godfrey was treating it as. He was in the middle of fierce combat.

"Get ready to meet your maker, Blobulor!" Godfrey shouted as he brought the stick down onto the head of his opponent.

Over and over and over again.

"Is he . . . ?" Carly asked.

"Yep," Rosa said. "He's fighting straw."

Hay, to be more accurate. Godfrey's opponent was a bale of hay. It was cylindrical and wrapped in plastic that was painted green, except for two sharp red eyes and a snarling, gaping black mouth. Arms made from lacrosse sticks protruded from the sides but offered little defense from the walloping. The hay creature had no feet, only a bulbous body that met the ground. Thus the name: Blobulor.

"You will live to fight another day, Blobulor," Godfrey said, stepping back to catch his breath. "But mark my words, my grievances remain. I shall smite you one day and smite you good."

It was safe to say that Godfrey was aware he had an audience. Otherwise, there would've been no reason for him to speak as loudly as he did. And when he turned toward the other three, who were standing at the entrance of the tennis court, he didn't seem the least bit surprised by their presence.

"Hey, Godfrey," Carly said. "We catchin' you at a bad time?"

With a mighty thump, Godfrey thrust his stick straight down onto the court, and then leaned on it as he peeled off his chain mail hood with his free hand. "You are catching me at my very best time. For you have witnessed my formidable might."

It should go without saying that Godfrey didn't speak like a typical sixth-grader. Or a typical person, for that matter. From as far back as Brewster could remember, Godfrey had always been different. In elementary school, there wasn't a day that went by when he didn't wear pajamas or a costume of some sort. Some of it was of the typical superhero/video game variety. A lot of it was self-made, with puffy sleeves, dazzling capes, and impractical shoes.

Teachers asked him to save his "dressing up" for the special events in school, the Fridays near holidays when they had pizza parties and such. But he didn't listen. "This isn't dressing up," he told them. "This is who I am."

His parents supported him wholeheartedly, sometimes even showing up to school board meetings in Renaissance-themed costumes. The officials eventually threw up their hands. Godfrey was who Godfrey was, and so long as the attire wasn't vulgar, they let it slide.

This always annoyed Brewster. Not because he felt Godfrey got preferential treatment—he was mocked more than he was celebrated—but because Godfrey often acted like he *deserved* preferential treatment.

He was special. You weren't. That was his attitude.

And Rosa appeared to be buying into it. As Godfrey put forth his ridiculous proclamations about "formidable might," a rumbling laugh emerged from deep inside her, surprising everyone, even Rosa herself.

"You okay?" Brewster asked.

"Yeah . . . it's just . . ." Rosa wiped a hand across her face and regained her typical composure. "He's perfect."

Godfrey's eyes narrowed. "Perfect for what?"

"I want to show you something," Rosa said, and she motioned for everyone to sit.

Curiosity won the day, and they all settled down opposite Blobulor. Rosa rested her phone against the monster's plasticky torso. It sat sideways, landscape view, for a more theatrical experience, and Rosa tapped at it until she successfully brought up a video. From its thumbnail image, Brewster instantly recognized it.

"Why are you showing this?" he asked.

"Because Godfrey should see it," Rosa said as she pressed the play icon.

It was one of Brewster's videos. Ten seconds long, his standard running time. It was called "Bad News/Good News." If there had been a screenplay for it, it would've been written like this:

INT. DOCTOR'S OFFICE—DAY
A simple room: white walls, wooden chair, table, and desk. A **DOCTOR** (confident and wise) with a white coat and a stethoscope confronts a **PATIENT** (sickly, with a greenish hue to his skin).

                    DOCTOR
                (somber)
        I have bad news and good
        news.

                    PATIENT
        Give me the bad news
        first, doc.

                    DOCTOR
        You're gonna die
        tomorrow.

                    PATIENT
        Oh my god, what's the
        good news?

                    DOCTOR
                (excited)
        The good news is, I'm
        not!

The Doctor does a happy dance.
                              CUT TO BLACK

In the video, Brewster was playing both parts, but through the magic of camera angles and editing, he was having a conversation with himself. And it looked seamless. While it wasn't the favorite of his videos, Brewster was proud of his accomplishment. The critics, however, had some thoughts.

"That was . . . not good," Godfrey said.

Even though he rarely cared what Godfrey thought, Brewster was suddenly flustered. "What? It was . . . I was—"

"You mean the acting?" Rosa asked Godfrey.

"Indeed. If you could call it that," Godfrey said.

"Writing too," Carly added. "I've heard that joke before. Or a version of it. I guess this video is . . . what's it called? Plagiarizing?"

"It's not . . . That's not . . . You can tell an old joke and . . ." Brewster could hardly get the words out. He could barely breathe.

"Watch it again," Rosa said as she tapped the volume icon and muted the video. "Without sound."

Brewster had seen the video countless times, so watching it had little effect on him. Watching the others watch it, however, was exceedingly difficult. Especially after hearing what they said about it the first time. Those next ten seconds felt like a minute. Or an hour. Or maybe a decade. (Though Brewster had only experienced one decade so far in his life, so that was perhaps a bold comparison.) It felt like a long time, in any case.

When it was over, Rosa tapped her phone back to the home

screen and spoke. Brewster expected her words would deflate him even more, and yet . . .

"It looks amazing, doesn't it?" she said.

Which felt better.

At least until Godfrey spoke. "A matter of opinion."

"No, it's a fact," Rosa said. "It honestly looks professional. Better than a lot of similar TikTok stuff. The editing is natural. The camera seems to be in the right place. Brewster has a real talent for directing."

"But not for plagiarizing," Carly said.

"Or acting," Godfrey added.

"That doesn't matter. Because you'll be doing the acting," Rosa told Godfrey.

"I'll be what?"

"We're making a movie trailer," Carly said. "And we have a role for you."

"Two words," Rosa told Godfrey. "Dark. Wizard."

Godfrey thought for a moment. Then he finally asked, "Can he be called Palivar the Pitiless?"

Rosa turned to Carly. Carly shrugged: *Sure, why not.*

Then Rosa turned to Brewster. It had been less than an hour since Brewster had rolled out of bed without a single thought of Godfrey or dark wizards named Palivar the Pitiless. It had been less than a day since Rosa had showed up with a five-thousand-dollar promise and turned his production of a ten-second video into something far more ambitious and anxiety-inducing. It had been less than a week since he had dug a hole and asked Carly to fall into it. In other words, Brewster had not sacrificed much. At this point, walking away wouldn't have been a big deal. Perhaps it would've even been the best thing for him. It certainly would've shielded him from more ridiculous criticisms from people who were supposed to be following their director's lead.

Yet he stayed. And he even asked Godfrey what would turn out to be a most ridiculous question.

"Do you have a good costume?"

Chapter 9

Don't Hate the Cosplayers

Costumes!

There was a room in Godfrey's house dedicated to them. Not just a walk-in closet. An entire room! Which was saying something because his house was not large. He, his parents, and his little sister, Isolde (aka Izzy), lived in a ranch-style home set back on a small wooded plot not far from the abandoned tennis court. It contained three bedrooms, but Godfrey and Izzy shared a bedroom so that the costumes could have their own dedicated space. And the costumes needed it. The room was barely big enough for all of them, and the family was constantly adding to the collection.

Godfrey led Brewster, Carly, and Rosa from the tennis court directly to his house and the costume room, pausing only briefly to greet his parents, who were on hands and knees tending to an herb garden in the front yard.

"My companions require disguises and regalia!" Godfrey announced while ushering the kids through the front door.

"Hear, hear!" his father bellowed, his voice echoing through the lavender-scented home.

Three metal garment racks lined the costume room, creating six rows of outfits. While the rest of Godfrey's house was quite messy, with bric-a-brac stacked on every available surface, this corner of it was pristine. It was like a miniature Halloween store, or something you'd find on, well, a movie set.

Godfrey rested his wooden stick against the edge of a rack, then carefully removed his chain mail, folded it up, and deposited it in a cubby that was marked with a sign that read "Armor and Medieval Miscellany."

"Like, I don't know you that well," Carly said to Godfrey as she ran a hand across a billowy green dress. "And this could just be a Vermonty thing that I don't get yet since I'm still kinda new. But is the reason you talk so funny because the costumes make you talk that way? Or do you wear the costumes to match your weird talking?"

Maybe this should've offended Godfrey, but it didn't. Instead, it inspired him to pull a cowboy hat from a shelf above a garment rack. He placed it on his head, angling it so that it was theatrically crooked.

"Ever hearduvtha Six Flags Shootout Spectacular?" he said,

using what could best be described as a cowboy voice.

"That's, like, a ride?" Carly asked.

"That there was a stage show," Godfrey responded. "My parents was cowpokes in it. It's where they met. And where they rustled up this here hat."

"So?" Brewster said, because that didn't explain anything.

"Soooo," Godfrey said as he took the hat off and placed it gently back on the shelf, retiring the cowboy persona with it. "They got engaged while waiting in line at the premiere of *The Lord of the Rings: The Return of the King.* And they got married at the Bread and Puppet Theater in Glover."

"I'm not sure I understand," Carly said.

"I was born in a tent while they were at the New Hampshire Ren Faire. And Izzy was born in the back of our van in the parking lot to Higher Ground before a They Might Be Giants concert."

"Still don't—"

"This is who we are," Godfrey said plainly. "It's in our blood, our souls, our very being. We celebrate the arts. We perform. We cosplay. Always have, always will, no matter what."

It felt like he had said this before. Countless times. Maybe it was originally his parents' line, and he was parroting it. Yet it sounded genuine. Like a person of faith talking about their religion.

Brewster's family had no religion, of any kind. Like many,

they exchanged gifts at Christmas and did the whole basket thing at Easter, but Brewster had never set foot inside a church or temple or mosque. Which by itself wasn't all that weird. He didn't know a lot of kids who went to services with any regularity. But those kids still had family traditions.

Brewster's family had none. They didn't hold regular game nights or go on annual camping trips. They didn't get portraits taken together or even throw the occasional neighborhood barbecue with packs of kids and dogs, overflowing coolers, and boisterous games of cornhole. Sure, his parents were social, and so was Jade. Just not as a family. And while they had some inside jokes that they shared—like the one about Brewster's mom always forgetting the names of simple things like kitchen appliances ("the thing that gets food really hot really quick")— they were never going to team up and dress as the Incredibles for Halloween.

Which was okay. Which was more than fine. Or at least that's what Brewster told himself. He'd been telling himself that for so long that he had no choice but to believe it. His family wasn't like other families, and that was what made them . . . special? No. Perhaps that wasn't the best word. Because it didn't feel special. *Unique* was a better word. His family was unique, and Brewster preferred to simply accept it, rather than dwell on whether it was a good or bad thing.

Similarly, the Tarkingtons were unique, but in a completely

different way. Brewster was, at least for now, thankful for that. If only because it meant he had free access to all these costumes.

"Show us something for Palivar the Pitiless," Brewster told Godfrey.

"Gladly," Godfrey said, pulling a black hooded cloak from a rack. "I have dark leather boots too, and I could attach a purple ball to the end of my quarterstaff. Voila! Spells and incantations!"

Flecks of silver shimmered on the cloak as Godfrey pulled it over his shoulders. Brewster took note. With the correct lighting, it would look fantastic on-screen.

"What about me?" Carly said, pushing costumes to the side, rifling through them like this was a clearance sale. "You got anything that—*AAAAAAAH!*"

Carly screamed because she saw something.

Brewster jumped back into a wall of fake swords because he saw the same thing.

A head poking out from the garment rack!

"Izzy!" Godfrey shouted. "What are you doing?"

Eleven-year-old Isolde Tarkington, with her explosion of curly red hair, had been hiding in the costumes, and Carly's frantic search had revealed the girl. With a look of wild glee on her face, Izzy said, "I know the perfect dress for you!" Then she hopped out and joined the group.

"Please ignore my sister. She's prone to shenanigans," Godfrey said with a sigh.

"He means I'm a pain in the butt," Izzy said, and she twirled once in place. "But I'm also hilarious!"

"That remains to be seen," Rosa said.

Brewster certainly recognized Izzy. She was hard to miss. And it wasn't only her hair. She didn't wear costumes quite as much as her brother, but she always wore multicolored outfits. To put it simply, she cosplayed as a rainbow.

In a flash, Izzy had pulled a dazzling dress off the rack. "This one's too big for me and too small for my mom, so you can borrow it. Are you going to a con or something?"

"We're making a movie," Carly said, grabbing the dress and examining it.

Rosa corrected her. "A trailer."

"You have to make a movie first to make a trailer," Izzy explained. "That's sorta how it works."

"Exactly what I thought," Brewster muttered.

"This dress is *amazing*!" Carly cried, stepping into it and pulling it up over her body. It swirled with radiant galaxies and nebulae. Stars and constellations were spread across every inch of its fabric. It was an entire universe that she could wear.

"Yeah, I thought it might look fantastic on you," Izzy said. "You're so pretty, you know?"

Carly was not immune to flattery. In fact, she welcomed its infection into her body, let it course through her veins until her eyes were wild and wide.

"We're gonna need to set some scenes in space!" she announced.

"Hey, hey, hey," Brewster said. "Slow down. Easier said than done."

But Rosa was having none of it. "We don't need easy, Brewster. We need good. And we don't need to slow down. We need to get going. Like, *right now*."

Godfrey, now adorned in his shimmering cloak, raised the hood over his head. "Agreed," he told them in a deep wizard voice, and he grabbed his quarterstaff and pointed with it to the door. "We shall discuss the proceedings in my chambers."

Everyone, except for Brewster, seemed thrilled by the suggestion. He wasn't sure why they wanted to get things moving so quickly. Simply excited? That was encouraging, but as the group (including Izzy, who followed at a distance and peeked in from the hall) moved from the costume room to Godfrey and Izzy's bedroom, Brewster worried that they were skipping over some important steps.

● ● ●

The bedroom was like the rest of the Tarkingtons' house—packed to the gills with oddities and collectibles. Sure, there was a set of bunk beds in it, and yet it felt less like a bedroom and more like a store. A curiosity shop, perhaps? Brewster had heard that term before somewhere and thought he had an idea of what one would look like. That idea was *this*.

Toys from multiple eras posed on shelves. Wigs and masks and hats perched on Styrofoam heads, or soccer balls, or even mannequins. Neon signs, and paper lanterns, and glass balls with plasma lights, like you'd see in a mad scientist's lab. A cauldron. A cauldron? A coffin? A coffin! It was resting against the wall and closed. And presumably housing a sleeping vampire.

When they entered, Rosa made a beeline for a display of Funko POP! Fortnite figurines and pulled one down. She picked Raven, a black-cloaked, black-hooded, red-eyed warrior. Godfrey cringed but didn't say anything, and Brewster resisted the urge to roll his eyes. It wasn't like Raven was still in the box. It might have been part of a set, but it was meant to be handled.

"We should start shooting in this room!" Carly announced. "It's like a whole—"

"We have to finish the script before we can do anything else," Brewster said, butting in. He'd been wanting to say that all morning, but it had been *rah-rah-rah, full steam ahead* all day, so he had assumed that no one would listen.

But Rosa listened. Tossing the Raven figurine gently to herself like it was a baseball—and earning more cringes from Godfrey—she stared at Brewster and asked, "Okay, what else needs to happen first?"

Brewster wasn't entirely sure. He'd learned about the preproduction of movies from the special features on some

Blu-rays his dad owned, so he had a vague idea. Rosa wasn't interested in vague ideas, though. If she was going to be an effective producer, she needed a solid plan. Even if he didn't know a lot, Brewster clearly knew more than everyone else, so he took it upon himself to provide one.

"Along with the script, we need equipment," he told her. "Cameras, lights, microphones, that sort of thing. We need to figure out where we're going to film. That's called location scouting."

Rosa gave Raven a firm squeeze, which Brewster took to mean she was happy with his answer. "Okay, then, you'll finish the script," she told him. "Godfrey will supply the props and costumes and makeup. Carly, do you have a bike?"

"Um . . . yeah," Carly said, posing like she was holding on to invisible handlebars. "Skating isn't my only skill. I'm incredible in multiple ways."

"Good," Rosa said. "Ride around. Find places to shoot. If it's on someone else's property, get permission. Tell them we're making a masterpiece, and they'll understand."

"What about you?" Godfrey asked Rosa. "Is it your job to simply boss us all around? Or do you intend to steal our collectibles as well?" In a series of quick motions, he snatched his Raven figurine out of the air and then returned it to its perch.

Brewster knew that Rosa was not one to back down from an insult or an insinuation, but he wasn't sure if she had a temper or not. Now was perhaps the time to find out.

Fortunately, Rosa kept her cool. Calmly but firmly, she told Godfrey, "I will be getting equipment and doing other *producer* things that only I can do. As for everyone else? You better finish your jobs so that when we meet again tomorrow morning, we're all working toward the same goal."

"Which is?" Godfrey asked.

Brewster couldn't help himself. Before anyone else could answer, he blurted out, "A million views."

Because that was it, right? That was what it all came down to for him.

A million views.

For Rosa, it seemed to be about the money. For Carly, perhaps the fun. Or the fame? He wasn't sure yet what the biggest draw for Godfrey was, other than a chance to show off his costumes. But for Brewster, it was about hearts and minds. It was about eyes! It was about that number below the bottom of every YouTube video.

Views. A million of them. That was the point when people truly noticed, when Brewster could hold his head high and declare that not only did he matter, but he would continue to matter. The world would remember him and what he had done.

His videos had never come close to a million views. But now there was funding. And talent. And suddenly, amazingly, it didn't seem like something that could only happen in a dream.

Chapter 10

The Dreaded Blank Page

They didn't stay much longer at Godfrey's house. Rosa sent them all off to accomplish their tasks. Brewster was relieved because he needed some time to himself. When he arrived home, he grabbed his phone and laptop, poured himself a tall glass of chocolate milk, and retired to a chair on his back patio.

On his phone, he read Carly and Rosa's description of the trailer over and over again until he had memorized it. Then he opened the document that they had started earlier. He put the cursor at the end of the text and pressed the delete button until there was just a white screen. A blank page.

He closed the laptop, then set it and his phone down on a small table. He turned his chair to a position where he could gaze out at the lush mountains rising on the horizon. From his vantage point, with the line of green peaks as a backdrop, the hole in his yard seemed insignificant. Which it was. There was hardly any depth to it. A crawling baby could escape it, no problem. It could hardly be called a hole at all.

Thinking big had never been a problem for Brewster, and yet he realized now that he had to think so much bigger if he wanted to achieve anything worth noticing. Sometimes he'd read about filmmakers who'd made their first movies on tiny budgets and then some studio would hire them to make hugely expensive blockbusters, like Marvel and Star Wars sequels. Some of the directors could pull it off far better than others could.

What was the key to the successes? Brewster didn't know. But he was certain that healthy doses of inspiration couldn't hurt. So he spent the morning leaning back in his chair, eyes closed, imagining. Pictures started to emerge on the dark canvas of his mind, enveloping his head in a very distinct mood. He sipped his chocolate milk. He listened to the sounds of nature and the road. The birds and the wind and the dog walkers and the cars. He waited patiently for some unseen power to take the images in his head and feed them. Grow them. Big. Bigger. Colossal!

It seemed to work. His mind swirled, and before long Brewster had a very distinct idea of how the trailer should look and sound. With his head positively bursting, he felt ready. So he hurried to his room.

He sat on his bed with his laptop and the blank page. He stared at it for a while but didn't type anything. He had all these images and sounds and scenes in mind, but he wasn't sure where to start. Action? Dialogue? A calm moment? Some foreshadowing?

Perhaps he needed a momentary distraction to get the juices flowing. He noticed that there was a pile of dirty laundry in the corner. Since fourth grade, his parents had put him in charge of his own laundry, and the weekend was usually when he did it. It was the weekend now. Why not grab a laundry basket and get to work?

A few minutes later, as the washer was sloshing the clothes and working the detergent into a froth, Brewster noticed his room was, as his father might put it, "an absolute sty." It needed to be cleaned too. He started that task next.

In the middle of cleaning his room, Brewster became hungry for lunch. There was leftover pizza in the fridge that he piled on a plate, reheated in the microwave, and ate at the breakfast bar. As his mom passed through the kitchen, she told him, "I liked your friends. It's good to have friends."

"They're just girls," was all Brewster could think to say in response.

"Even better," his mom called out as she bounded upstairs.

When lunch was over, Brewster had to put his laundry in the dryer and then get back to tidying. So that's what he did.

Of course, folding the laundry was essential, as was putting it away. And the room obviously needed some finishing touches.

Dusting. Straightening. Alphabetizing books by author. Therefore, it was already well into the afternoon when he returned to the laptop and the blank page.

"Okay," Brewster told himself. "Time to get to it."

He got to something else instead. IMDb.com, where he watched the trailers for some of his favorite movies. *Necessary research*, he told himself.

That necessary research led to more necessary research. Screenplay formats. Editing apps. Special effects tricks. Suffice to say, Google got a workout that afternoon and rabbit holes led to other rabbit holes. Reading about ravens led to reading about the basics of falconry led to reading about the art of tapestry, and Brewster eventually found himself perusing the Wikipedia entry for the Battle of Hastings.

Huh? What the heck was that? Well, it was an important battle in the year 1066 that changed the course of history in England, France, and beyond. But what did it have to do with *Carly Lee and the Land of Shadows*?

Absolutely nothing. Interesting, though.

As Brewster was reading about crossbows and swords, his mom popped into the room with a bag of tacos for dinner. Somehow, the day had passed into evening.

"You're hard at work on something again, huh?" she said, placing the bag on his bed.

"Um . . . obviously."

"I'll be out in the barn tonight if you need me," she told him as she left. "Don't stay up too late."

"Don't worry," he called out. "I'm almost finished."

It was the whitest of lies, but Brewster still felt bad about it. Not because he was lying to his mom, but because he was lying to himself. Almost finished? He hadn't even started yet! Distractions had gotten the better of him. Even now, as he clicked back to the blank page, he was compelled to look away. His gaze drifted to an open window.

The sun had dipped and was casting an orange and purple glow across the lawn. This, in filmmaker's terms, was known as the golden hour. There were obsessive directors who insisted on shooting their movies exclusively during the golden hour. It made the images ache with beauty, and while it was an extreme demand, Brewster had to respect such dedication to the craft.

The light of the golden hour looked particularly lovely on Jade, who, dressed in their favorite blue hoodie and a long red gingham skirt, was waiting in the driveway. Brewster simply watched them linger for a while, until a car erupting at the sunroof with arms and hollers pulled up, and Jade hopped in. Off the teenagers went, laughing into the dusk.

A few moments later, Brewster's mom made her way from the house carrying a box of supplies for refinishing some old furniture she'd found along the side of the road. She lugged it, and an old boom box, out to the barn, and with the doors wide open, she turned on a CD and got to work. The sounds of jangly guitars and the fumes from the wood stain wafted through Brewster's window, so he finally decided to close it. The blinds too.

Enough procrastination.

Enough lying to himself.

Brewster had the vision living up there in his head. It was finally time to yank it out and put it on the page. For that, he needed concentration. Full concentration. Turn-off-the-Wi-Fi levels of concentration.

Since Jade was long gone and the music in the barn was playing from a CD, Brewster knew he could unplug the router without hearing wails of dismay. He could also turn off his lights, so that nothing in his room would lure him away from his task. So that's exactly what he did. Until there was nothing but the boy and the glowing expanse of the page.

And then, only then, in the dark, alone with his thoughts and his keyboard, he finally typed. A slug line.

INT. CARLY'S BEDROOM—MORNING

Something close to magic happened next. The words arrived. Scene headings. Dialogue. Action. It all started flowing.

INT. CARLY'S BEDROOM—MORNING

A cool room, with lots of cool stuff in it. Gorgeous light breaks through an open window. A breeze blows the curtains. **CARLY LEE** (12 and heroic) shuts the window and turns to an unseen companion, whose **VOICE** we hear from off-screen (OS).

> CARLY
>
> I'm not used to the sun anymore. I've got to go back.

> VOICE (OS)
>
> Where?

> CARLY
>
> To the land of shadows.

EXT. DARK SKY—NIGHT

Clouds rush across the sky. Ravens too. A title card flashes across the screen:

A ROSA BLAKE PRODUCTION

INT. BORING CLASSROOM—DAY

Carly sits at a desk, daydreaming. Her **MEAN TEACHER** (old and gross) uses a book to point at her. He's very intimidating.

MEAN TEACHER

Eyes on the whiteboard, young lady!

Carly looks up at the whiteboard, but suddenly it's not white. A dark stain spreads over it like black ink on a blank piece of paper. Carly jumps up.

>   **CARLY**
>   Am I the only one who
>   sees that?

Probably. Because her **CLASSMATES** (bored or nervous) shrug.

EXT. THE HOLE—THE GOLDEN HOUR

The sun is going down behind the mountains and making the world orange and purple. Carly stands next to a hole in her yard. She steps forward like she's about to jump into the hole.

>   **CARLY**
>   Here goes nothin'!

She jumps.

The clack of the keys. The emergence of dark letters on a bright page in a dark room. The thrill of creation coursed through everything . . .

INT. ENCHANTED FOREST—DAWN

EXT. CAVE OF THE SHADOWZOIDS— NIGHT

INT./EXT. COLORFUL VOID BETWEEN DIMENSIONS—WHO KNOWS

Carly climbs a ladder as mist swirls around her.

The Sprite hops down from the trees.

Palivar the Pitiless stands atop a tower and shoots lightning bolts from his wizard's staff.

The Snidious Nurk plummets, hits the ground, and explodes into black goo.

CARLY

There's a strange force in this realm.

CARLY

Home. I can make it home. I know I can. I know. I know. I know . . .

PALIVAR

You! Shall! Be! Smited!

Title Card:
CARLY LEE AND THE LAND OF SHADOWS

76

Brewster had to stop so he could breathe. He was typing so fast, the words bypassing his brain and going directly to his fingers. What might've seemed to be a standard fantasy or action adventure felt intensely personal to him. It didn't make him cry, but it almost made him cry.

BZZZZ!

His phone vibrated on the dresser, snapping him back to the real world. It was past eleven o'clock, and Brewster never got messages this late. Maybe it was Rosa? She seemed like the type who might break the basic rules of civility.

But no, it was from his dad.

> Finally here with Laura! I've missed her soooo much.

The message was accompanied by a picture of his dad embracing a woman who was kissing him on the cheek. They appeared to be standing next to a bar dimly lit by strings of colorful Christmas lights. Brewster didn't recognize the woman.

BZZZZ!

Another message from his dad.

> Sorry bud. Meant to send that to someone else. Feel free to delete. Sleep well.

That was it. No other explanation.

Not that Brewster needed one. He was accustomed to

ignorance when it came to the lives of his parents. For instance, he didn't know what they did at their jobs. He knew where they worked and what titles they had, but if someone had asked him what tasks his mom and dad performed during the day, he'd be stumped. Of course, things would've been easier if they were teachers or firefighters or something the entire world understood, but that didn't matter to him. He simply wasn't interested in that aspect of their lives.

This picture felt different, though. It was of interest to him. Not because it seemed wrong, necessarily. While his mom was far from touchy-feely, his dad was often physically affectionate. In fact, with friends and even some acquaintances, he was a full-on hugger and cheek-kisser. But there was something about this picture that felt like . . . more.

Was this more than a kiss? More than a friend? More than Brewster cared to think about? It was the last one, for sure. So instead of responding, he deleted the messages. Then he set his phone facedown on the bed, closed his eyes, and whispered to himself, "Not my concern. Not my problem. Not going to be distracted again."

The first thing he saw when he opened his eyes was a page full of words on his laptop, and he convinced himself it was better to concentrate on something he could control. So he started typing again.

Focusing. Rewriting. Revising. Honing. Perfecting.

Chapter 11

Premature Preproduction

On Sunday morning, Brewster drank coffee. He'd never tried it before, but he knew it was good for people who didn't sleep much, and he hadn't slept much. There was some left over in his mom's French press, so he filled a mug and took a swig and—

No. Sorry. Not for him.

The rest of the mug went down the sink, and Brewster grabbed one of Jade's Diet Cokes from the fridge instead. He chugged it, and then tried to crush it in one hand, like he'd seen people do, but it only dented the can a little. Lack of sleep was to blame.

With a bundle of stapled copies of the script under his arm, he headed outside. The grass was wet with dew, but the sun was already climbing fast and drawing the moisture back into the atmosphere. Brewster had expected to find the others already there and hard at work, but he was alone.

Ever since he started middle school, alone was how he liked to do things. Team sports? No way. Group projects at school? Yikes. And while he sometimes asked other kids to star in his productions, he saw that as a necessary annoyance. He often wished he had the skills to simply create digital actors instead.

For the first time in a long time, he felt different. He felt, not excited exactly, but *ready* to see the others. For the first time in a long time, he didn't have an overwhelming desire to be alone.

And he wasn't alone for long. Piper Barnes was suddenly there. She was returning from her customary morning bike ride, gliding into her driveway on a bike that used to be Brewster's.

To be clear, it hadn't been Brewster's bike for very long. It had been Jade's bike, but when Jade had outgrown it three years before, they had passed it along to Brewster. Brewster knew how to ride a bike, but he wasn't much interested in it. So one day when Piper asked if she could borrow it for a quick trip to the park, he told her she could have it. Forever.

"Thank you, thank you, thank you, thank you," she had said as she hugged him and then hopped on the bike and rode around in tight, happy circles in her driveway.

"It's so old I'm not sure I could've even sold it," Brewster said with a shrug. Because if he could've sold it, he probably would've. Still, it felt good to see her so happy.

It also meant he could avoid awkward conversations with his

mom about "going on adventures with other kids" and "exploring your independence instead of another corner of the internet." Brewster knew that if he ever wanted to use the bike as a prop for a video, he could always ask to borrow it back for an afternoon. But he never found the need.

Besides, Piper used the bike constantly. Every morning she went out for a ride, sometimes even towing one of those two-wheeled baby trailers behind her. She had picked it up at a yard sale, filled it with heavy books, and used it as part of a training regimen designed to improve her endurance and hill-climbing speed.

Piper wasn't towing the baby trailer on this particular morning, but she had obviously gone through an intense workout. Sweat poured from her brow as she hopped off the bike. Her face was as red as the stripes on her sneakers. When she saw Brewster, she nodded a hello, took a few steps closer, and panted out some words.

"Everything . . . okay . . . with you?"

"Sure. Why wouldn't it be?"

She wiped her brow, took a long, deep breath, and replied, "No reason. Sometimes that's something . . . you should ask people."

Brewster wasn't sure if he'd ever asked anyone that, and he wondered if he should return the sentiment. But he decided not to, because what if everything *wasn't* okay with her? What would he do then? Did he know how to help a teenage girl through life's ups and downs?

The answer was a solid no, so he changed the subject. "We're making a movie over here," he told her. "And around the neighborhood. If you see us doing anything weird, don't, like, call the police or anything."

Piper considered this for a moment, and then in a serious tone, she said, "Don't let them use you, Brew."

"What do you mean?"

"Your voice. It's vital. Protect it at all costs."

Her tone was even more serious now, like she was the head of an intelligence agency detailing an important mission. Brewster didn't want to disappoint her, so he said something he didn't really mean. "Thank you. That's helpful advice."

It wasn't that he didn't believe her advice. It was that he didn't fully understand it. His voice? Really? He wasn't a singer.

"I'm always here if you need me," Piper told him, and then she turned and wheeled the bike back to her garage.

Like so many of his interactions with Piper recently, this one left Brewster with an uneasy feeling. He was missing something. And the biggest problem with missing something is you usually don't find out what that something is.

● ● ●

Brewster's family had a barn. Which wasn't as odd as it might sound. Lots of people in his neighborhood had barns because lots of people lived in old farmhouses. The barns weren't filled with livestock or hay. They housed kayaks and winter tires, garden tools and trash cans, essential things and things that didn't fit in the house and should've been thrown away long ago but were pushed into damp, cobwebby corners because maybe, just maybe, they'd be of some use someday. Those things were rarely of some use on any day.

Brewster's family's barn wasn't quite so cluttered. His parents had even converted one part of it—some old stables—into a seasonal entertaining space where they'd hang out with other adults who either didn't have kids or left their kids at home. The space had chairs, a bar, smart speakers, a coffee table for setting out hors d'oeuvres. Brewster rarely spent time there, partly because he preferred his couch and 4K TV, but also because it didn't feel like a family space. It felt like an extension of his parents' life outside the family. It was a comfortable spot, though, and perfect for a preproduction meeting. That's where Brewster headed after talking to Piper.

By the time he had spread copies of his script across the coffee table and positioned some of the chairs around it, the others arrived.

"Welcome, welcome," he announced. "There's a script for everyone."

As Carly grabbed hers, she took in the surroundings. "Is

everyone in Vermont a farmer, or do they all secretly want to be?" she asked. "Not sure if I'll ever get used to this weird little state."

"Brave little state," Godfrey said as he grabbed his copy. "That's what many people call it."

Carly flopped down in an old armchair. "I'm certainly brave to be the new kid around here. Hanging out in barns and pretending like it's normal. I swear . . ."

"Less talking, more reading," Rosa said as she grabbed her copy and shook it in the air. "Let's see how Brewster did."

The others agreed by not objecting, and as soon as nearly everyone was seated, they silently looked over the pages. Izzy had joined them too, in the role of Godfrey's assistant, but she was standing at a distance from the other four and taking notes on an iPad.

Carly read her pages with top teeth to bottom lip, head tilted, and eyes narrowed. She spoke first and sounded only mildly disappointed. "It's . . . pretty okay, actually."

Was that a compliment? The tone might not have sounded like it, but the words kind of did. Whatever it was, Brewster would take it. After the reaction to his "Bad News/Good News" video, "pretty okay, actually" felt like a glowing review. And it was followed by even better ones.

Godfrey sighed and said, "It's *quite* okay."

And Rosa added, "It'll definitely do." But then she smiled

after saying it, which made it feel like the best news of all.

"I worked really hard on it," Brewster said.

"It shows," Rosa said firmly.

"I worked hard on my duties as well," Godfrey announced. Then he snapped his fingers and shouted, "Isolde! My portfolio, please!"

Izzy hopped to it. She was wearing a shoulder bag, and she immediately opened it and removed a small digital projector, tethered by a long braided cord to an iPhone. "Where's your screen?" she asked Brewster.

"My screen?" he responded.

"For outdoor movies, video games, that sort of thing."

"Oh. I don't have one."

"You mean you actually watch things *inside the house* during the summer?" Izzy said. "How very weird."

Was it? It didn't feel weird to Brewster. Though he could understand the appeal of having an outdoor movie screen. Or even one in his barn. It was dark in there and the wall was made of pine, so the wood was relatively light like a movie screen.

"You can probably project things on the wall," Brewster told them.

"If we must," Godfrey said, grabbing the projector and phone from his sister and positioning them on the coffee table. In moments, a blurry image appeared on the barnboard, and with a few tweaks to the projector, Godfrey brought it into focus.

It was displaying the Instagram feed for an account called @TarkingTonsOfFun, and the first pic was a series of words written in a swooping font. They read: GODFREY TARKINGTON'S MENAGERIE OF CINEMATIC ENSEMBLES.

Godfrey held up the phone and said, "We are about to go on a journey, my friends, into a world of masquerade."

He tapped the phone as he flicked it like a magic wand and a new image appeared on the wall. It was a photo of Izzy, and she was wearing what looked like an aviator's costume: leather hat with goggles pulled up to the forehead, a puffy-sleeved white shirt with a leather vest over it, and pants with lots of buckles.

"Our steampunk heroine can pilot a zeppelin or laser blast a top-hatted villain," Godfrey said. "But can she resist the temptation of Lord Gearsworth?"

"Hmmm," Rosa said, thumb to chin.

Godfrey tapped and flicked the phone again and brought up another photo. This time it was a picture of himself, but he was wearing pale makeup, prosthetic pointy ears, and a flowing green robe. "The elf king Renvinor is one thousand years old, but is only at the beginning of his life. In elf years, he's basically a baby. But a baby with infinite wisdom and a magical connection to the forest that no mortal man can even fathom."

"Elves basically live forever," Izzy added. "I saw it in a movie once."

Carly rolled her eyes. "Well, if you saw it in the movie . . ."

It was on to the next slide.

"Here we have the Porcinipine!" Godfrey boomed. "'Tis a beast so fearsome that—"

"Stop!" Brewster shouted as he jumped in front of the projected light and the image of a bulbous, quilled, piglike mask settled across his body. "What are you doing?"

"What I was asked to do," Godfrey said. "I'm presenting the costumes and makeup that will be in the trailer."

Brewster held up his copy of the script. "But none of those characters are in here."

Godfrey shrugged. "Right. Because I only read it a few minutes ago. Which means you should change it."

The suggestion raised Brewster's eyebrows so high that they nearly touched his hairline.

Carly started to put up her hand, but like in school, she didn't wait to be called on to speak. "I'm not sure if my locations match your script either, Brewy. Is that gonna be a problem?"

"Where are your locations?" Rosa asked.

Carly swirled her arms around. "Um . . . everywhere?"

The group was silent for a moment, until Rosa said, "You didn't do your job, did you?"

Carly didn't appear the least bit bothered. She simply tapped her noggin with a finger and replied, "I did all the research up here. I think we should go wherever we want, whenever we want, and see what happens. You know, wing it?"

"No," Brewster said, the image of the Porcinipine still cast upon his body. "No. No. No. This isn't about winging it. This is planned. This has a script."

Carly jumped up and poked at Brewster's chest, hitting the Porcinipine right between the eyes. "This whole thing was *my* idea, okay? I thought it up in the first place. Which means I have a say too, you know? All you wanted me to do was fall in a hole. I'm better than that."

"She's better than that," Rosa echoed.

"See?" Carly said, backing away and standing next to Rosa.

"But he's better than that too," Rosa added. "Let's figure this out, because everyone is confused."

"Yeah, I'm confused because why haven't we started shooting yet?" Carly said with a dismissive snort.

"Because we don't have the right costumes or locations yet," Brewster said. "I don't even see the equipment."

Now Rosa was on the spot. For perhaps the first time ever, Brewster saw a crack in her stony demeanor. "I don't have them today, but I'll have them soon. Don't worry."

"Then what are we here to do, exactly?" Godfrey asked.

Izzy looked up from her iPad. "You could rehearse."

Chapter 12

We Have a Few Notes

"How's this gonna work?" Carly asked as they stood in the yard next to the hole. The sun was intense, and so Carly was wearing sunglasses. The others were using their hands as visors. Carly looked a little cooler than the others. Not unlike, for lack of a better word, a star.

"It'll be the same as with the other video," Brewster told her. "You say your lines, and I'll provide direction."

"Yeah, but there isn't much to say," Carly said, shaking her script in the air. "It's a trailer, so it's either a few words or nothing at all. I'm screaming or battling a bunch of monsters or whatever for most of the time. Then it moves onto the next thing. Why can't we figure that all out when we're shooting? What's the point of rehearsing?"

"To make sure that your performance is ready and we don't

waste time when we are ready to shoot," Brewster said. "There are a lot of different ways to scream. Or to battle a bunch of monsters."

"In order to get a feel for our personas, I would recommend that we do some character work first," Godfrey said.

"Why?" Carly responded. "My character doesn't have a job. She's basically me. And I don't have a job."

"That's not what I mean by character work," Godfrey said. "We can find the essence of our characters by getting to know them. By asking questions."

"Such as?" Carly asked.

"*Who* is your character?"

"Me. Carly Lee. Duh. We know this already."

"Where are you from?"

"Um . . . here. Or New Jersey originally. Jersey girl to the core, baby!"

"And what do you want?"

"To stop answering your questions."

"Fine," Godfrey said. "Maybe it'd be better if someone asked *me* the questions instead."

Rosa did the honors. "Okay, who are *you*?"

Godfrey puffed up his chest, and his voice dropped a couple of octaves. "My given name is Palivar H. Crivengourd, but I have studied and mastered the dark arts, and my ruthlessness has bestowed upon me a dreaded title known throughout the universe. I am Palivar the Pitiless."

"Where are you from?"

"I was born deep in the belly of a cave, on a moonless night, in the Land of Shadows. My mother raised me in darkness until I could summon fire on my own. My father fed me only amphibians, so that I was comfortable on land or in water."

"You eat toads?" Rosa asked.

"Maybe salamanders," Godfrey said. "I'm improvising. Go with it."

"What's your favorite TV show, Palivar?" Carly asked with a smirk.

"I suspect you mean television program?" Godfrey said in his Palivar voice. "I have no interest in such things. I'm too busy dedicating myself to more fulfilling pursuits."

"Such as?" Carly asked and then she started to mock him by dancing. "Dabbin'? Flossin'? Startin' the new TikTok craze?"

With a wagging finger, Godfrey whispered, "Never. My one and true mission is . . ." Then he paused for a moment, before thrusting that finger skyward and shouting, "To destroy Carly Lee!"

Carly stopped dancing, covered her eyes with a hand, and snickered in pity. But Rosa nodded and said, "I like this. This could work. Brewster, can you change your script?"

"Um . . . maybe?"

"Good. Because Godfrey's character should talk more like

how Godfrey is talking, and Carly's character should sound more like she sounds."

"Are you giving me a note?" Brewster asked.

"I don't know," Rosa said. "Is that something producers do?"

The answer was yes. Definitely. Always. Producers were notorious when it came to giving notes. Notes were, of course, suggestions for changes in scripts. Sometimes, if a producer had natural creative instincts, the notes were helpful. But often they were nonsense, based on nothing more than a producer's desire to remind everyone who was in charge. And they would do that by changing something, anything.

For instance, a producer might give a helpful note, such as "This scene is a little long and features a lot of dialogue. Can you trim it and let the characters' actions and emotions deliver more of the plot?"

On the other hand, a different producer might say, "There's too much emotion in this scene. An audience would rather laugh than cry. I know this is a serious drama, but could you add a talking monkey? You know, to lighten it up a bit? People go wild for talking monkeys!"

What did Rosa's note qualify as, then? To Brewster, it qualified as an insult. He had worked so hard on the script. He had stayed up all night! Now she wanted him to change it?

"Producers do what they want because producers control the money," Brewster told Rosa. "But *great* producers know what's best for the movie. Artistically, I mean."

"And that's what I mean," Rosa said. "We have two actors who are good in different ways. We should take advantage of that."

It wasn't a bad point. It might have even been a good point, because there was no denying that Godfrey had a talent for getting into character. But it meant more work for Brewster, and it meant his original script was somehow inadequate. Which bothered him.

It didn't bother anyone else, of course. They had moved on to other things. "You do realize there are more than two parts in the script, right?" Izzy told everyone. "And we only have two actors."

This was certainly true. The script had at least four other characters, not to mention all the magical creatures.

"My sister simply wants to play a part. Pretend she isn't here," Godfrey said, which caused Izzy to make a sour face. "We have plenty of wigs and costumes to aid our transformations. Not a problem."

"Wait, now I have to play more than one part?" Carly said.

"I thought that was obvious," Godfrey said. "You play the female parts, and I play the male parts."

"That sounds like a lot more work than I signed up for," she said.

"Yes, but I know you can pull it off," Rosa said.

Once again, Brewster felt the need to take charge. Because if he didn't take charge, someone else would. He was the director, after all. Taking charge was part of the job.

"I have no problem with Izzy playing a part," he said. "Actually, maybe we should audition other kids too."

"Or maybe you and Rosa should slap on some makeup and learn some lines," Carly said with a smirk.

Brewster wasn't opposed to acting. He'd always played a role (or two) in his own productions. Rosa, however, held her palms up in protest. "No way. Not me."

"But you'd be perfect for the Mean Teacher character," Godfrey suggested as he waved his script.

"The Mean Teacher is described as old and gross," Rosa said with her hand on her chest.

Godfrey shrugged, which was unsurprising because he rarely thought of anyone's feelings but his own. However, Carly shrugged too, and that puzzled Brewster. Carly could certainly be full of herself, but she wasn't cruel. Plus, Rosa was Carly's good friend.

Or was she?

Earlier, the girls had been defensive when Brewster claimed they weren't friends, and he had accepted that maybe he was wrong about them. But what if he wasn't? What if they were lying? He didn't know why they would lie, but it was starting to seem like a possibility. Because they sure didn't act like friends.

Especially now. Friends are supposed to have each other's back. He knew this. After all, he used to have friends.

Used to is perhaps too strong a term. He had never technically lost any friends. Still, it had been a while since he had spent much time with any. There had been a group of guys from elementary school: Tyler, Henry, Elijah, and Luke. And there had been playdates and birthday parties. Fort building and Minecraft. Soccer and sledding. But by middle school, Brewster started seeing less and less of them, which was mainly his choice. All he wanted to do was make videos, and while they enjoyed making videos, they wanted to do other things as well.

They were still school friends. He could sit with them at lunch if he wanted, pair up with them in gym class for tennis or whatever. But he rarely did. Too often they talked about things he wasn't much interested in—mountain bikes, skiing, girls—and they were only humoring him when they listened to Brewster carry on about his passion for videos. They were good guys. Just not *his* guys anymore.

Still, he seemed to have more in common with them than Carly and Rosa had with each other. If he were ever in a jam, he knew that at least one of them would help him out. He would do the same for them. In fact, he would do the same for Rosa. So that's what he did.

"How about this for a note?" Brewster said. "The teacher in the script doesn't need to be old and gross. I can change the description. I can say she's . . . I don't know . . . wise."

Rosa's eyes narrowed. "You think I'm wise?"

Brewster *did* think she was wise, but for some reason he said this instead: "I think you could play someone who is wise, yeah."

Rosa considered this for a moment, and then said, "Still not for me."

With her copy of the script rolled up and tucked in her pocket, Carly announced, "Well, it's been fun, but I already know who my character is, and little Izzy here can handle my wardrobe, so I don't think I'm needed anymore. There are rails and ramps calling my name, and you can do the same when you're ready to start shooting."

"You're leaving?" Brewster asked.

"You bet," Carly said as she headed toward her skateboard. It was resting against the barn, its jet-black deck adorned with a bright green map of New Jersey.

Rosa stared at Carly as she left. Brewster couldn't tell if Rosa was mad or not, but if she was, she wasn't saying anything to stop her "friend." And so he didn't say anything either. Carly skated off down the road, her wheels whirring and clicking and crunching on the gravelly pavement.

"She's a real diva, isn't she?" Godfrey said as soon as Carly was out of earshot.

Brewster knew that divas were usually considered good performers, but he also knew it wasn't necessarily a flattering term. Defending Carly wasn't his top priority, though. "I don't care what she is," he said. "We need to focus on the script for now. Consider it our bible."

"That's true," Izzy butted in to say. "But you also need to make a shooting schedule. Some storyboards wouldn't hurt. You need a script supervisor and a line producer and a budget accountant."

Rosa's stare now shifted to the eleven-year-old clutching the iPad to her chest. "What did you say?"

"I did some reading last night about making movies," Izzy told her. "Brewster has been right about a lot of stuff, but there's other stuff too. Making schedules and handling budgets and—"

"You're hired," Rosa said.

"Huh?" Izzy replied.

"You know about that other stuff, so you can handle that other stuff. Okay?" Rosa said.

Izzy nodded enthusiastically. "Yeppers."

"Wait," Godfrey protested. "But she's my assistant!"

"Not anymore," Rosa told him. "We'll all meet at recess tomorrow. At the pirate ship. Be ready."

And just like that, rehearsals were over.

Chapter 13

Gorilla Style

Brewster got ready. With a little time to reflect on it, he realized that Rosa was right about the script, and for the rest of Sunday, he revised the dialogue so that the characters sounded more like Carly and Godfrey did in rehearsals. He also did the location scouting that Carly had neglected to do, walking through the neighborhood, taking pictures with his phone, even asking his neighbor Mrs. Boddington, an elderly widow with a pair of snarling German shepherds, if they could film in her immaculate flower garden. She agreed, but told him to bring treats, to "get on Wilhelm and Wolfgang's good side."

On Monday, recess couldn't come soon enough. During his morning classes, Brewster would sneak looks at his script while the teachers weren't paying attention. When he passed the others in the hall, he wanted to talk, but he knew there wasn't time, so he simply cocked his chin and pointed at them, the universal sign for *this is gonna be great!* At lunch, he ate as quickly as possible, so that he would be near the front of the pack when it was time for recess.

When recess did finally come, Rosa managed to sneak ahead of him and stake her claim on the pirate-ship structure that took up the northeast corner of the playground. Brewster hurried up on deck and slipped her a new copy of the script as he sat down next to the ship's helm. "Latest and greatest," he said.

She read it quickly, nodding as she did, a good sign. When she finally looked up at him, she used her firmest voice. "It's ready."

"Good. Are you?" Brewster asked.

Rosa rolled her eyes, then opened her bag. She pulled out a small movie camera with a long zoom lens, as well as a few microphones and LED lights.

"Whoa," Godfrey said as he joined them. "That's fancy stuff."

"The best stuff," Rosa said. "Two thousand dollars' worth."

"What!" Godfrey shouted, drawing the gazes of fellow classmates and recess monitors.

Rosa immediately started stuffing the equipment back into her bag. "Shh. I don't want it confiscated. I'm not even supposed to have my bag out here."

"What's being confiscated?" Izzy asked as she climbed

up onto the pirate ship. "Candy? I hope it's candy. If it is, I'll confiscate it first."

"Fantastic," Godfrey said with a groan. "Little sis has arrived. Why are fifth-graders allowed to have recess at the same time as sixth-graders? It's unconstitutional."

While the comment seemed to bounce right off the perpetually sunny Izzy, Brewster wasn't so dismissive. "Why are you always so hard on her?" he asked.

"Do you have a little brother or sister?" Godfrey asked.

"No."

"Then you couldn't possibly understand," Godfrey said. "But let's get back to that outrageous number. Two thousand dollars!"

Rosa shushed him with a finger to her lips and whispered, "Yes. And I need Izzy to account for that in the budget. We should have a little over three thousand dollars left."

"Three thousand dollars!" Godfrey shouted.

"Shhh!" both Rosa and Brewster said.

"It's a lot of money is all," Godfrey said. "I think my parents' van is worth about that much."

"Less," Izzy said. "Definitely less."

"Before you start getting dollar signs in your eyes, you gotta know that all the money is going toward the production. No one is getting paid," Brewster said firmly.

"Unless we unionize," Izzy replied.

"What does that mean?" Brewster asked.

Izzy thought for a moment and then said, "Don't worry. I don't think it'll come to that."

Rosa had stopped paying attention to the conversation. Her focus was now on the camera, the only piece of equipment that she hadn't returned to the bag. Instead, she had positioned it on the edge of the pirate ship so that the lens was pointing toward the playground.

"The reason we're here is to start filming," Rosa said as she tapped on the camera's touchscreen. "Right now, for instance."

"Don't we need Carly first?" Godfrey asked.

"She won't be joining us," Rosa said as she twisted the lens slightly, zooming in on something. "She's busy."

This was true. Carly was busy . . .

Busy risking her life!

In the middle of the playground, she was walking across the top of the monkey bars with the balance of a circus performer. Arms out, head high, feet on the rungs. Kids were cheering her on, while Ms. Neilson, the recess monitor, was hurrying over to put an end to things. Rosa's lens was poised on the young acrobat. All the action appeared in the camera's viewfinder as the record icon flashed red.

"Does she know you're filming her?" Brewster asked.

Rosa shook her head.

"So why are we filming her?" Godfrey asked.

"To capture the authentic Carly Lee," Rosa told him.

By this point, the authentic Carly Lee had climbed down from the apparatus and Ms. Neilson was leading her to the other corner of the playground to have a little chat. Carly raised a triumphant fist as she went, which was a huge hit with the crowd.

"Pretty useless to film if it's not in the script," Brewster said, trying hard to deny that the footage was probably quite compelling.

"It doesn't cost anything to shoot," Rosa said as she grabbed the camera and handed it to Brewster. "And there are some scenes set in school. So why don't you take over? You're the director, right?"

The camera was slightly heavy. Cold to the touch. And absolutely glorious! Boy, did it feel great in Brewster's hands. While it wasn't much bigger than a loaf of bread, it was colossal compared to Brewster's phone, which was what he used to shoot all his videos. He wondered if this was what it would feel like for Carly to hold a professional's skateboard, or for Godfrey to hold an authentic medieval sword.

"I can use it?" he asked. "For real?"

"Just don't let anyone see," Rosa said. "Hide it in your backpack. Keep the zipper open and get whatever footage you think we need."

"Guerrilla filmmaking," Izzy said. "Sweet."

"I'm not a gorilla," Brewster grumbled as he scrolled through the options on the touchscreen. Filters, zooms, shutter speed, frame rate: it was all here. Not that he knew how to use most of those things. He set it to auto mode until he had time to learn.

In the meantime, Izzy laughed at him. "Guerrilla filmmaking is a style of making movies. Realistic. On-the-fly. Sometimes using actors who don't even know they're in a movie."

That made more sense, of course. It also gave Brewster an idea. The night before he had changed a character in the script from Mean Teacher to Wise Teacher, so that Rosa would play the part. But now he realized it might make sense to change it back. After all, he had a mean teacher. Mr. Warburton. For social studies. Which was their class right after recess. The trailer would look so much better with an actual adult playing the role, along with "actors who don't even know they're in a movie."

"I think we might actually be able to shoot a scene. Next period. Gorilla style or whatever. Do you think we could somehow get Mr. Warburton to say, 'Eyes on the whiteboard, young lady'?" Brewster asked.

"Stands to reason," Godfrey responded. "He basically says it every day."

"True," Brewster said. "But we need Carly to say her lines too."

"If she knows she's on camera, she'll do it," Rosa said. "I'll go tell her."

Unfortunately, that would be difficult. Because Ms. Neilson was now escorting Carly into the school.

"Oooh, looks like she's in real trouble now," Izzy said, her hands clasped together in delight.

"Great," Rosa grumbled. "Even if Carly does show up to social studies, how are we going to explain that you're shooting?"

Brewster may not have known everything about making movies, but he knew that there was one way in which all movies were like all videos. Things rarely went to plan. Weather, sickness, injuries, any number of factors could change a production suddenly. The best directors were the ones who adjusted.

Was this the first production where the star didn't know she was appearing in the scene because she had gotten in trouble on the playground and had missed the preproduction discussion about guerrilla filmmaking? Yeah, probably. But that didn't mean there wasn't a solution to the predicament.

That camera felt so natural in Brewster's hands. He was ready to do this. In fact, he *had* to do this.

"Okay. I can work with what I have," Brewster said, and he stuffed the camera under his shirt. "Follow me."

The crew disembarked from the pirate ship and marched confidently toward the back entrance to the school.

Chapter 14

The Warburton Factor

Brewster arrived in the classroom first, before even Mr. Warburton, who had been on his lunch break. This was good. This was essential to the plan.

While he was alone, Brewster captured some footage of the room. Shots of the walls, windows, and the whiteboard. Rosa and Godfrey stood guard in the hall, keeping any other kids at bay with warnings of an angry wasp on the loose. When they saw Mr. Warburton rounding the corner, Godfrey whistled, which was a signal for Brewster to get a move on.

Brewster appeared at the door ten seconds later, flashing an OK sign. "Coast is clear," he whispered to the others. "And we're rolling."

Only one other kid in the crowd heard him. But it was the worst kid to hear him. Liam Wentworth, Brewster's biggest fan and the guy who was always there when you didn't want him to be, poked his head through the door and asked, "Rolling? Does that mean you're making one of your—"

Brewster thrust a hand over Liam's mouth and glared at him. "I meant I rolled over the wasp with a . . . a . . . a ball."

Oh man, Brewster thought. *Is that the best I can do?* But Liam nodded like he understood, and it seemed to convince the rest of the crowd.

"So did you crush it?" their classmate Morgan Lutz asked.

"Oh, he's crushin' it, all right," Rosa said as she spotted Brewster's backpack lying on his desk with the camera lens barely poking out through the slightly open zipper. She patted Brewster on the shoulder and stepped inside. Then the rest of the kids followed in her wake.

Brewster slowly removed his hand from Liam's mouth, and Liam, instead of complaining, smiled, winked, and made a motion like he was locking his lips with a key. Brewster trusted him, because Liam was the type of guy who always kept his word, but it still made him uncomfortable.

When Mr. Warburton entered, he addressed the class. "I suspect you were all lingering outside my room so you could discuss the three branches of the United States government. Is that correct?"

"Definitely," Rosa said. "I'm a Judicial stan myself."

"Legislative," Godfrey said.

"Come on, it's Executive all the way," Liam said, winking at Brewster.

"It's what, now?" Carly asked as she appeared in the doorway.

Relief! The star was here! Now all they had to do was explain to her that there was a camera hidden in a bag and they were shooting the trailer guerrilla-style. Easy, right?

"I've got something to tell you," Rosa whispered to Carly as they made their way to their desks.

Mr. Warburton did not, however, condone such socialization. "Class has begun, people," he said. "We can save the chitter-chatter for after the bell." Then he motioned for everyone to sit.

They did as he asked. Mr. Warburton wasn't cruel, but he was strict and consistent in doling out consequences, and every kid knew it. It was always best to do as he said. Former students—usually college-age or older—often stopped by his room between classes to thank him for being such a talented and dedicated teacher. They called him their "favorite," which puzzled his current students, because they usually reserved that word for the teachers who cracked jokes, or showed videos in class, or shared special high fives with each of their students.

To Brewster and his peers, Mr. Warburton was too intimidating to be a favorite. His class was too difficult. And though they clearly learned things in it (the three branches of the US government, for instance), no one looked forward to it.

But that's what made the class perfect for the trailer. The

extras didn't have to act bored or nervous, as they were described in the script. They were naturally that way. Mr. Warburton was authentically intimidating, and at some point, he was bound to say his line, "Eyes on the whiteboard, young lady," because he said it all the time. Especially to Carly.

Yet, for some reason, as Mr. Warburton started his lesson, Carly's eyes were planted firmly on the whiteboard. No daydreaming. No napping. No goofing off. She was engaged in ways Brewster had never seen from her before. She raised her hand and waited to be called on. She answered questions, though not always correctly.

To get as much footage as possible, Brewster rotated his backpack a few times, focusing the camera on various students and Mr. Warburton. But for the extended period it was pointed at Carly, she was doing the opposite of what he needed her to do.

Brewster was tempted to pass her a note—*Dear Carly, please be bad or lazy!*—but it seemed too risky. The backpack itself hadn't aroused any suspicions because Brewster often kept it on his desk during class. But Mr. Warburton had a keen eye for any student leaning over, whispering, or causing anything that resembled a distraction. His eye was especially keen for kids who weren't paying attention.

So when Brewster noticed that Rosa, who was usually quite attentive, had her head on her desk and was practically asleep, he knew what was coming. He swung his backpack and the camera toward Mr. Warburton just in time to catch the teacher turning from the whiteboard, pointing at Rosa with the book in his hand, and saying, "Eyes on the whiteboard, young lady."

Winner winner chicken dinner!

As Rosa sprang to attention, she winked at Brewster. She had obviously done this on purpose, baiting their teacher into saying the line.

Ingenious!

Carly gave Rosa an odd look: *What's the deal?* And as soon as Mr. Warburton turned back around, Rosa mouthed the words *we're filming*. And she pointed to Brewster's backpack.

It took Carly a few moments to put the pieces together. But when she did, her posture straightened. With frantic fingers, she fixed her hair. And with a subtle tilt of her head and a wiggle of her eyebrows, she told Brewster what to do: *Turn that camera over here, buddy.*

He got the hint and slowly rotated the backpack until the camera lens was on their star.

That's when she jumped into action. Literally.

In a flash, Carly was on her feet, pointing at the whiteboard and shouting, "Oh my dear god! Does anyone see the horror?" Then she slapped her hands on her cheeks, and her jaw dropped. It was an improvised version of the line, but Brewster didn't necessarily hate it.

The entire class responded with puzzled looks, which was

what they needed. Brewster rotated the backpack and camera to capture their reactions, but when he did, he swung it too fast, causing the lens to poke out through the zipper.

"What on earth is going on here?" Mr. Warburton said, hurrying over to Brewster's desk. He seized the camera before Brewster had a chance to squirrel it away. In fact, Brewster didn't even try to hide it. He froze, and he remained frozen while Mr. Warburton examined the camera with the careful attention of an archaeologist examining an unearthed artifact.

"That's mine," Rosa said. "I was letting Brewster borrow it."

Mr. Warburton looked up from the camera and asked, "Were you recording the class?"

Brewster couldn't lie. He knew that lies piled onto more lies, and that a mountain of lies was a dangerous mountain to climb. So he responded with a soft, "Yessir."

Mr. Warburton nodded and took the lens cap, which was dangling on a string, and gently placed it back over the lens. He didn't return the camera to Brewster, though. Or Rosa. Instead, he carried it to the front of the room and placed it on his desk.

"Brewster. Rosa. Carly. Here. After class. Understood?"

Perfectly. They nodded but didn't say anything. There was no denying that they were in deep trouble.

● ● ●

When the bell rang and the other classmates left, Mr. Warburton motioned for Brewster, Rosa, and Carly to approach his desk.

"I won't ask you to explain yourselves," he said as he picked up the camera. "I think I know exactly what's going on."

"You do?" Brewster asked.

"I do," Mr. Warburton said. "You thought that if you recorded the class, you wouldn't have to pay attention or take notes. That you could all watch the video together later during a study session. Is that right?"

Again, Brewster couldn't lie, even with a nod. But Carly certainly could. "That's exactly right, sir," she said.

"And *you*," he added while pointing at Carly. "*You* were trying to distract me with your ridiculous theatrics."

"I'm not sure they were 'ridiculous,' but yeah," Carly said. "Guilty, guilty, guilty."

He slowly handed the camera to Rosa, and said, "Do you mind if I tell you kids a story?"

"Do we have a choice?" Rosa asked.

Of course, they didn't. Because Mr. Warburton simply started telling it.

"When I was your age, I had a teacher named Ms. Monroe. Now, Ms. Monroe had been my father's social studies teacher, maybe even my grandfather's. She was that old. But she was good. And tough. She knew her lessons inside and out. And she knew what students had to learn in order to succeed.

"I was struggling in her class, mostly because my hand

couldn't take notes fast enough, so I had the brilliant idea of bringing a cassette recorder to school. Figured I'd record the lesson, give my hand a rest, and review the material at home. Well, that wasn't the wisest of choices. Ms. Monroe spotted the recorder sticking out of my bag and not only did she confiscate it, but she yanked the tape from the cassette. Disemboweled it, right there in front of my eyes."

"That sounds bad," Carly said. "Is disemboweling bad?"

"Yes," Mr. Warburton said. "It usually is. And what I'm trying to tell you is that I could've removed the data card from your camera. I could've snapped it in two. But I didn't. Do you want to know why?"

"Because you're . . . nice?" Rosa said.

Mr. Warburton shook his head. "Because I'm not one for theatrics, Ms. Blake. And it's what Ms. Monroe did next that was more important."

"Smash the tape player too?" Carly asked.

Mr. Warburton sighed. "What she did next was she gave me an extra-credit assignment. She told me that if I was so enamored of recording things, then I should use my skills to give something to the world. Not to simply make a copy of her lecture."

"So did you do the extra-credit assignment?" Rosa asked.

"You better believe I did. A radio show. *Warburton in the Morning* is what I called it. I read the news, gave a weather forecast, played some of my favorite tunes. And when I gave the tape to Ms. Monroe a week later, she listened to it. And she gave me a B."

"Only a B?" Brewster said.

"That's what it deserved. But the grade didn't matter. It's what I learned that mattered. I had a tool. That tape recorder. And since I was privileged enough to have that tool, then it was my duty to use it. To its fullest capacity. And that's what I want from you. That camera you have there isn't a toy. It's a tool. Use it to its fullest capacity."

"What do you mean?" Brewster asked.

"Do you know what a documentary is?" Mr. Warburton asked.

"Sure," Carly said. "It's like a movie, but boring."

"Some are, I'll give you that," Mr. Warburton said. "But they're also part of an education. I'm going to propose something, inspired by the late, great Ms. Monroe. How would you like to make a documentary?"

"Will it get us out of trouble?" Carly asked.

"This is not a bribe, Ms. Lee. This is an opportunity. And do you want to know what you get out of opportunities?"

"Money?" Carly asked.

"Not from documentaries," Rosa grumbled.

"You get experience, and with experience comes confidence, which is better than money," Mr. Warburton said.

Carly didn't lack confidence, at least as far as Brewster was concerned, so he expected her to tell Mr. Warburton as much. But instead, she asked, "What should the documentary be about?"

"That would be entirely up to you."

"If it was going to be about school, would you give us permission to shoot in school?" Carly asked.

"I would. And I'd inform other teachers of the project. But, and this is a big but, you need to show me that you are ready for this responsibility."

"And how would we do that?" Rosa asked.

"You *tell* me you're ready for it."

"That's it?" Carly asked.

"Your word is your bond," Mr. Warburton said.

Carly looked at the other two. Rosa said, "Yeah," but Brewster remained stone-still, so Carly made the decision for him.

"We're ready," she said.

That's all Mr. Warburton needed to hear. "Then I wish you good luck. I look forward to learning more about the project, but I don't want to hold you any longer. Off to class. I'll check back with you by the end of the week."

With a wave of his hand, he sent them on their way.

Chapter 15

We'll Fix It in Post

Light-headed and foggy eyed, Brewster stumbled as he followed the two girls out of Mr. Warburton's room. Godfrey was waiting in the hall for them, and when he said, "So is this the end of the line?" it broke Brewster out of his temporary daze.

"I don't think so," Brewster said, like he could hardly believe it himself. "I think we just agreed to make *two* movies now."

"How's that?" Godfrey asked.

But Brewster didn't answer him. He was too busy pointing a finger at the girls. "You lied, and you included me in your lie."

"No," Rosa said. "We got you filming privileges in school, on school time."

"To make a documentary!" Brewster shouted. "When will I have time to film the trailer if I'm, I don't know, interviewing lunch ladies? And am I supposed to be working on this after school too? This messes up everything!"

Carly checked her flanks to make sure no one was listening. "Chill out," she whispered. "You're not making any documentary."

Brewster shrugged her off and said, "But we have to report back to him. What are we supposed to tell him? I can't lie to him."

"You won't have to," Carly said. "Let me handle it."

Producers were supposed to handle such things, so Brewster looked to Rosa to take over. But she was too busy gushing about what they did earlier. "I can't believe you figured out we were filming," she told Carly. Your ad-lib was perfect."

"Hey, if the camera is on me, I'm gonna give the camera what it wants," Carly said as she fluttered her eyelashes. "Speaking of. We should watch it. Like, right now."

"But it's time for math," Godfrey told her.

"Okay, then after school," Carly said. "My place. We have a big TV."

This was an irresistible invitation, so there would be no arguing with the star. They were back in her good graces, and she was back on board for the shoot. So at least one good thing had come out of the Warburton fiasco.

● ● ●

Later that afternoon, they followed Carly from the bus to her place, a short walk up a steep hill to a collection of drab town houses that were mostly second homes for people from New York or Boston who visited in the winter to ski, or in the summer to hike.

The whole crew was there. Brewster, Rosa, and Godfrey, of course, but also Izzy, at Rosa's insistence. Before ushering them inside, Carly stopped at a row of black metal mailboxes, inserted a key into number twenty-four, and pulled out a stack of envelopes. She sifted through them, saying, "Junk, junk, junk . . . Jersey return address, oooh!" She pocketed a small envelope and tossed the rest into a blue recycling pail.

Using a different key, she opened the door to town house number twenty-four, and shouted, "I have guests!" as she entered.

"I'd like to meet them!" a voice shouted back.

A man emerged from a back bedroom into the main living space of the town house. He was shirtless and wearing board shorts, a trucker hat, and sunglasses. He didn't really look like a dad to Brewster. Too young. But he also seemed too old to be a brother. He was probably in his late twenties or early thirties, though Brewster wasn't the best at guessing ages.

"Hey, Ken," Carly said. "Where's Mom?"

"Shopping," he said. "Or working. Who knows?"

"What are you doing?" she asked.

"You know, just chillin'," he said. "Played some *Breath of the Wind* all morning. Might go paddleboarding later."

"Nice," Carly said. "Me and my friends are gonna watch

some stuff on TV. And it'd be cool if we're not disturbed."

With a fingertip, Ken inched the sunglasses down a tad, so he could peer out over the top and shoot her a suspicious look. "Nothing rated R . . . or worse?"

Carly cracked up. "That's hilarious. Not even close."

The same fingertip tapped the sunglasses back into place, and Ken said, "Good enough for me. Some top-shelf parenting from yours truly. Time to hit the reservoir. Later, kids."

"Water is still pretty cold," Carly said. "Don't fall in."

He flashed her a two-fingered salute, then sauntered past the bunch, nodding his goodbyes. However, he stopped when he saw Rosa.

"Oh hey, Rosa," he said. "Say hi to your folks for me, all right? Tell 'em I loved that beet salad from last Saturday. Gonna need the recipe."

Rosa hung her head and mumbled, "Sure thing," as she tried to move out of his way. But he still managed to tousle her hair before he exited the town house.

There was silence for a moment and then Izzy asked, "Was that guy your dad?"

Carly cracked up again. "Ken's my stepdad. Or he has been for about six months. He was my mom's ski instructor a couple years back when we came here on vacation. Flash forward and suddenly I live in Vermont and we're a happy, happy family."

"Seriously?" Godfrey asked.

Carly shrugged. "Seriously. He makes my mom smile. And he's a nice guy. Nicer than my real dad." She said it with the same nonchalance someone uses when telling you which brand of salad dressing they prefer.

"Where should I go with this?" Brewster asked, holding up the camera.

"You probably know better than I do, but there are all sorts of spots to plug stuff into the TV," she told him as she pointed in its general direction, which was the only direction she needed to point.

The TV was huge! At least seventy inches. But it was resting on the tiniest media stand Brewster had ever seen. It was a veritable death trap for any toddler. Maybe even for Izzy, who was barely four feet tall. Brewster made sure to be extra careful as he commandeered an HDMI cord from a Nintendo and eased it into one of the ports on the camera.

"I'm making popcorn," Carly announced as she bounded to the other side of the town house. There were some appliances and a tiny counter over there, though it was a stretch to call it an actual kitchen. It basically bled into the rest of the living space, which was also a living room and a dining room and whatever else it needed to be other than a bedroom.

Brewster wasn't used to places like this. While the furnishings and style were all familiar, the arrangement felt exotic. It made him wonder what type of arrangement his parents might have if they decided not to live together. Would one of them live in the house while the other lived in a place like this?

No. He wasn't going to even consider that. To keep his mind off such thoughts, he kept to the task at hand. By the time there were popping sounds coming from the microwave, Brewster had everything synched and ready to play. Meanwhile, Izzy was tapping away on her iPad. Godfrey was walking around the room, examining the various decorations and wall hangings, as if he were in a museum. And Rosa was waiting patiently on the couch, legs crossed, hands in lap.

"Let the show begin!" Carly announced when she joined them. She was carrying cans of flavored seltzer and two big bowls of popcorn. Godfrey and Izzy took a bowl and found some seats on the floor, while Carly plopped down on the couch next to Rosa.

"Okay, let's see what we got," Brewster said, and he started the video.

The first shot was of Rosa's face, looking directly at the audience. "Testing, testing, one, two, three. Does this thing work?"

Carly winced. "Okay, that's definitely not going into the trailer."

"I had to try it out first, jeez," Rosa said.

"I know, I know, I'm just waiting on the—"

Carly dropped the handful of popcorn she was about to

munch back into the bowl, and she pointed at the screen and shouted, "Look at me!"

The footage of her walking across the monkey bars was shot from a distance, so her body was relatively small, but that's what made it impressive. The entire scope was in view, projecting a feeling of true peril. It was even more stunning because Carly was so smooth in her movements. Like a ballet dancer.

"Look at me, look at me, look at me!" Carly kept shouting as she bobbed up and down on the couch. But the joy didn't last because soon she was being led away by Ms. Neilson and the next set of shots were appearing on-screen.

Walls.

Windows.

Whiteboard.

"Please explain this boringness," Godfrey said.

"Oh, I get it," Izzy said. "Brewster was filming cutaway shots. For coverage."

"What's coverage?" Rosa asked.

"It's when you shoot a bunch of extra things and different angles that will help you later when you need to edit," Izzy said. "Brewster was shooting stuff in the classroom because he might cut it together with some action and dialogue in the trailer to give the audience a sense of the place. Amirite, Brewster?"

"Ummm . . . yeah," he said.

"He's obviously been studying like me," Izzy said.

Nope. Brewster had no idea they were called *cutaway shots*, and he didn't know the first thing about *coverage*. Not that he was about to admit that. He simply said, "Thanks, Izzy."

Then it was on to the main event, the secret footage shot in Mr. Warburton's room. As soon as it started, there were criticisms.

"Is that a zipper?" Rosa asked.

It was. The zipper from the backpack was an out-of-focus distraction on the left side of the frame. That didn't mean there wasn't a solution, though.

"We can crop it out later," Brewster said. "In post."

"Whoa!" Godfrey shouted as the image on-screen shifted violently, the result of Brewster swinging his backpack around during the shoot. "That was certainly jarring."

"Well, I couldn't stop the camera between shots, so we'll edit the moving part out," Brewster said. "In post."

"It's diagonal," Rosa said as the shot focused on Mr. Warburton. "Why is it diagonal?"

She was right, of course. The camera had tilted, and while Mr. Warburton was still in the frame, saying, "Eyes on the whiteboard, young lady," his head was in the top left corner and his body in the bottom right. It didn't look terrible. Unsettling was more like it.

"Were you going for a Dutch angle?" Izzy asked Brewster.

Huh? He knew a lot about videos and movies, but that term

might as well have been in another language. Dutch, perhaps. And his answer was basically the same as before: "We'll fix it in post."

As the shot finally turned to Carly, Brewster was prepared for more complaints. But, by some good fortune, this time the zipper was out of the way, the transition was smooth, and the framing was perfect. Carly looked great as she jumped up, pointed at the whiteboard, and shouted, "Oh mr mrr grdd! Rrr anyrrr see sst hrrr?"

"Um . . . why do I sound like that?" Carly asked.

"I don't know," Brewster said. "Maybe the microphone got covered up."

"Nothing a little ADR can't fix, right, Brewster?" Izzy said.

He wasn't even going to bother trying to figure out what she meant, so he simply agreed. "Yep. ADR will make it better."

"In post," Izzy added.

The shot continued until Mr. Warburton's hand came into the picture and grabbed the camera. A few seconds later, the screen went black. And that was it.

They all sat in silence for a few moments, until Rosa finally spoke. "So . . . is any of that footage usable?"

The answer was a shaky *maybe*. But Brewster needed the crew to believe he had this under control, so he said, "Of course. I'll have a rough edit of the classroom shots finished tonight. Don't worry. It will look professional."

It wasn't a lie so much as a ridiculous promise. How was he going to pull this off?

As Brewster considered his options (which were limited), Godfrey's finger shot up. "Eureka!" he shouted.

"You have an idea that will help the edit?" Brewster asked.

"No, this isn't about your silly edit," Godfrey said. "This is about the monkey bar shots. We can use those!"

"How so?" Rosa asked.

"Isn't there a moment in the script where Carly is hopping over lava on some stones?" Godfrey asked.

"You bet there is," Carly said with a smile.

"Well, all Brewster has to do is take the video of you balancing on the monkey bars and make everything around you disappear and then insert lava and rocks in the background. Ever see the end of *Revenge of the Sith*? Like that."

"Is that something you can do?" Rosa asked Brewster. "In post?"

Saying *no* felt impossible at this point, but Brewster could've at least said he'd need a few days to figure things out. But he wanted to project pure confidence, so he blurted out, "I'll have it done tonight."

"Nice," Carly said as she seized the bowl of popcorn.

And Izzy delivered one last bit of movie industry lingo: "I love dailies. They're so much fun. Can we do dailies after every shoot?"

Dailies. Another term none of them had ever heard. That hardly mattered. They got the gist.

"If dailies involve watching myself on this big screen while eating snacks, count me in," Carly said as she stuffed her mouth with popcorn.

Chapter 16

Truly Special Special Effects

Back in his room, alone again, Brewster got to work. It quickly became clear that his old MacBook and his outdated iMovie app might not be up to the task. But it wasn't like he had the money to upgrade them. Perhaps there was room in Rosa's budget. Could he ask her to buy him a new computer and the latest editing software? It seemed like a legitimate expense, but how much of the budget would that take up? She'd already spent $2,000 on camera equipment. A new MacBook and the right software might be another $1,000 to $2,000. Poof! There went most of the cash before they'd even really begun.

It was wiser to give it a shot with what he had. It took at least a minute for iMovie to load, never a good sign. But once the app was running, he was able to transfer the videos from the camera's memory card to the clip bin. Reviewing the footage one more time confirmed that this would be a tough job. The app featured an option to create a trailer using predetermined filters, edits, and sound effects, but he knew that was the easy route out and would come off as amateurish. He'd promised that this would look professional, so he did the things he told the others he would do.

He cropped.

He tilted.

He adjusted sound levels.

He toiled for hours until . . . he had about five seconds of somewhat usable footage.

Five seconds. Total.

At this rate, he'd never finish the trailer. Five seconds was about 3 percent of the trailer's proposed running time of three minutes. And he hadn't even attempted the special effects. He still needed to add the growing inky blackness to the whiteboard. Which was to say nothing of the monkey bars.

Carly's monkey-bar monkey business was perhaps the best piece of footage they had, but he couldn't do a thing with it. If they had put a green screen behind her, it might have been possible. But with all the colors and movement in the background, it wasn't as simple as using a magic lasso editing tool to make everything around Carly's body disappear. At least not without it then looking completely fake, like all those TikTok videos where people use filters to awkwardly superimpose their bodies over incongruous backgrounds.

If it were a still picture, he could've used Photoshop to cut out the background and add in the lava like Godfrey had suggested. But this was at least eight seconds of video. Each second of footage had twenty-four frames in it, which was another way of saying that for each second, there were twenty-four pictures to manipulate. Twenty-four frames times eight seconds was nearly two hundred pictures to fix. Plus, he had to figure out how to make a convincing background featuring fire and hot bubbling lava.

He closed the laptop. It was too much. He had made a promise, and now he had to break it. Telling Rosa would be the hardest part. She'd want him to solve the problem. She'd demand a backup plan. Which was annoying, but probably what you should expect from a good producer.

There was, of course, one other option. It would mean swallowing his pride, but it was better than facing Rosa. He would do something he was rarely comfortable doing when it came to the technical and artistic aspects of his work. He would ask for help.

He went to Instagram on his phone. He remembered that the account for Godfrey and Izzy's family was @TarkingTonsOfFun, so he typed it into the search box and found it instantly. Not only was it a showcase of their various costumes, but it was also a celebration of their trips to festivals and cons. Brewster had his own account that he never posted on (@BrewsterGoesViral), but that's all he needed so that he could follow the Tarkingtons and send them a DM.

This is Brewster Gaines. I don't know how to contact Izzy, but can you please have her contact me? Thank you.

Moments later, his phone rang.

"Hello?"

"What in the devil do you want with my sister?" Godfrey's voice came back, sounding like Brewster had never heard it before. Tough. Mean. Angry.

"Um . . . um . . ."

"Out with it, Gaines!" Godfrey shouted. "Why are you bugging Isolde!"

"I'm . . . I'm . . ."

Then there was laughter. Giddy and sustained. And not only from Godfrey. It sounded like his whole family was listening in on the call through speakerphone, and they were all cracking up.

"I'm playing with you, Brewster!" Godfrey announced. "It's called method acting. Staying in character. You know, being villainous. Like Palivar the Pitiless?"

"Oh," Brewster said, still confused, though a little less so.

"Anyway, here's Izzy," Godfrey said.

A giggly girl's voice was now on the other end, saying, "Director man! How can I help ya?"

It took Brewster a moment to regain his composure, but

when he did, he was remarkably honest. "I don't know what to do."

"That's okay," Izzy said. "No one does. That's what makes life exciting!"

"Maybe for some, but not for me," Brewster said. "You've been reading a lot about making movies, right? Have you been reading about special effects?"

"No," Izzy said. "But after I finish prepping for tomorrow, I can study up."

"Really?" Brewster said with a relieved sigh. "Because I need some help figuring something out."

"And help you shall have! We'll talk about it on the bus tomorrow morning. See ya then."

The line went dead. Brewster didn't even have a chance to say goodbye.

● ● ●

The next morning, Brewster didn't even have a chance to say hello. He was barely settled into his seat on the bus when Izzy appeared next to him, tapping him on the shoulder and saying, "Scooch over."

He did, but instead of Izzy taking the open spot, another girl sat down.

"Um, this seat is for—"

"It's for Harriet," Izzy said. "She's here to save the day."

Harriet Joseph, a small girl with big eyes and round glasses, looked up at Brewster and smiled. "I like to draw," she said. Evidence of this fact took the form of a sketchbook in her lap and her handful of colored pencils.

"That's . . . nice," Brewster responded.

"And she's great with digital graphics and—" Izzy put a curled hand to her mouth and made the sound of a trumpet (*ba-dada-dum!*) before announcing, "Special effects!"

Harriet flashed Izzy a thumbs-up, and then used her thumb to push her sliding glasses back up her nose. "She means I can do CGI. It stands for computer-generated imagery."

"I know what it stands for, but what's happening right now?" Brewster asked.

Izzy plopped into the seat across from them and said, "I read about special effects last night, and the main thing I learned is that if you need truly special special effects then you need someone who's good at creating truly special special effects. Therefore, I give you . . . Harriet!"

"Do you need truly special special effects?" Harriet asked with a grin.

Brewster wanted to tell her *no*. He wanted to say that he would handle it, that he simply needed a little more training. But then he peered down at her sketchbook, which she had opened, and he saw a gorgeous sketch of a movie poster.

It wasn't for a real movie, or at least not for one he'd ever heard of. The title was *MONSTERS AMUCK!* and the sketch looked like the poster for any blockbuster superhero or sci-fi film, with all the colorful characters crowded together. Only the characters in this poster were all monsters. Many were scary. Some were cute. But they were all wonderful and unique. Tentacles that tangled and curled and ended with menacing claws. Fur that glowed like fiber optics. Creatures with multiple mouths and tombstone teeth. Slime, dripping and oozing and promising supreme grossness. Wild eyes everywhere. Mangled ears. Bulbous knuckles. Cartoonish, and yet they felt real. Quite simply, art.

Brewster couldn't deny her talent or her desire to be involved. So he said the only thing he could possibly say: "Yes. I need truly special special effects."

Chapter 17

They're Called Call Sheets

And then there were six. Once again they met at the pirate ship during recess. This time Carly joined them, but she was clearly bored.

"Are we filming now?" she asked as she chewed on the drawstring of her hoodie. "Please tell me we're filming now."

"Not until after school," Rosa said. "But Izzy has something to share."

Izzy handed out sheets of paper to everyone. They looked like this:

Rosa Blake Productions www.rosablakeproductions.com Rosa's House		SNACK: 4:30 p.m. (provided) DINNER: 7 p.m. (provided) SUNRISE: 6 a.m.
Producer: Rosa @RosaBlake2006 **Director**: Brewster @BrewsterGoesViral **LP:** Izzy @TarkingTonsOfFun	**Carly Lee and the Land of Shadows!**	SUNSET: 8 p.m. WEATHER: 65°F, Sunny NEAREST HOSPITAL: UVM Medical Center Burlington * But if it's really bad, we should probably call an ambulance.

LOCATION	3 p.m.	ADDITIONAL NOTES
Brewster's Come on. We all know where that is.	Tuesday, May 14, 2019 Day 2 out of Who Knows!?!?	Godfrey will fetch costumes at our house while the rest of us work on the first scene.

SCENE	SET & DESCRIPTION	CAST	NOTES
Carly jumps in the hole	The Hole. You know, the obvious one in Brewster's yard. Like it says, Carly will jump in it.	Carly	Might need multiple changes of clothes because of the dirt.
Carly meets Palivar	Barn—the darkest part. Cobwebs? Bonus! Palivar emerges from the darkness. Carly screams. Spooky!	Carly Godfrey	Does anyone have a smoke machine? The script mentions smoke.
The Sprite shows the way	Tree. The crab apple behind the barn that's all twisted. A Sprite provides directions from her perch in the tree.	Carly Izzy	The script says there's a sunset in the background, so we'll time it for sunset.

CAST MEMBER	CHARACTER	CALL TIME	SPECIAL INSTRUCTION
Carly	Carly	3 p.m.	You're #1 on the call sheet!
Godfrey	Palivar	5 p.m.	Don't forget the makeup!
Izzy	The Sprite	7 p.m.	Yay! That's me!

"It's called a call sheet," Izzy said. "All movies use them. It's basically a way to tell everyone what we're doing when and who's doing it."

"Looks professional," Rosa said.

"I found a template online," Izzy said.

"Why is there a hospital listed?" Carly asked.

Izzy was nonchalant with her answer. "In case someone gets maimed."

That information lit a spark in Carly, and the look on her face hovered somewhere between joy and terror. Brewster thought it best to nip that in the bud. "No one is getting maimed," he assured them.

"Better be the case," Rosa said. "That's a director's responsibility, you know?"

"I know," Brewster said, because he did know. What happens on the set is always the director's responsibility.

But then Carly reminded him of something. "Okay, but when you and I were first doing your bottomless pit video, you said you couldn't guarantee I wouldn't break my arm."

This was also true. Though he'd forgotten he said that.

"Well, I can't guarantee anything *one hundred* percent."

"Sounds positively reckless to me," Godfrey remarked.

"Agreed," Rosa said. "Do you think maybe we need to hire a lawyer? Get some documents together. To be safe. Legally, I mean."

"No," Brewster said. "It'll be safe. I promise no one is getting maimed."

Get off my back! That was the reflex, the instinct that inspired Brewster's statement. But the promise wasn't as empty as it might've been in the past. The responsibility weighed on him. His biggest worry used to be about getting the perfect shots, and now, suddenly, it was about one of the actors, or crew members, being taken away on a stretcher. Whether he got a good shot or not didn't matter if someone got hurt. Or at least, it wasn't the only thing that mattered. If he wanted this to succeed—and he did want it to succeed—then he had to think about other people. What a concept!

"Does 'number one on the call sheet' mean something good?" Carly asked, pointing to the bottom right corner of the page.

"It means you're the"—Godfrey made air quotes—"*star*."

"Excellent. I was hoping that's what it meant," Carly said and then she folded her copy and put it in her pocket. "And since I'm number one, I have a request."

"Great," Godfrey said. "She's demanding a tour rider now, isn't she?"

Carly's face twisted in confusion. "I don't know what that is. All I want is the camera."

She held her hands out to Rosa. And Rosa asked, "For what?"

"For Warburton," Carly said. "He stopped me in the hall earlier and asked if we had started work on the documentary.

Gotta keep him off our back, right?"

Rosa considered, then relented. But rather than handing Carly the camera, she placed the camera's strap over Carly's neck. "Be careful with it," she said.

"I've only broken, like, five bones in my life, so odds are in our favor," Carly replied, then she turned away from them, the camera swinging out to the side and, thankfully, not hitting anything. "See you weirdos at three o'clock."

"But we're not done," Brewster said. "We haven't even introduced Harriet yet."

Carly swung back around and pointed at Harriet. "I'm guessing she's Harriet. I recognize her. Fifth-grader, right?"

Harriet nodded and smiled.

"Okay, that means we've met," Carly said. "Later, taters."

With that, Carly hurried over to the slide at the bow of the pirate ship. With one hand holding the camera to her chest and the other grabbing the bar above the slide, she swung her body, and in one fluid motion she slid away. But not before Harriet called out to her. "It was great to meet you, too!"

When Carly was gone, Godfrey fixed his eyes on Harriet. "What's your job, then?"

Harriet shrugged enthusiastically. "That's the fun part. I don't really know."

"Special effects," Brewster explained. "And graphics. And . . . other stuff. I know I promised to have the special effects done today, but to give them the most professional look, I figured Harriet's skills might help."

This seemed to satisfy Rosa, who stared at Harriet but didn't object. A good sign.

Godfrey, on the other hand . . .

"She's not getting involved in costumes, is she?" he said. "Or art direction?"

"Wait, are you the art director now?" Izzy asked her brother.

"I thought that was assumed," Godfrey said. "I also assumed I'd be the director of photography. I have the best eye for such things."

"But it's not on the call sheet," Izzy said, smiling devilishly as she tapped the paper. "The call sheet says you're going to our house to fetch the costumes. That's, like, a production assistant's job."

"That's because you wrote the call sheet, you nincompoop!" Godfrey cried, waving his arms theatrically.

Brewster had never fought with Jade like this: angrily, yet playfully. Sure, they had their disagreements, and maybe when they were younger, such things had been more heated. But they were nearly six years apart, which felt like an entire generation gap. The music and videos and memes that Jade liked were so different from the ones that Brewster enjoyed. Which meant that even though they rarely argued, they didn't usually have a lot to talk about. Did Brewster want more arguments? Not really. But listening to Izzy and Godfrey go at it made him curious about what that might be like.

"You'll do a call sheet before every day of shooting, correct?" Rosa asked.

"Correct," Izzy said proudly.

"Good," Rosa said. "It's helpful. But I think we *all* need to talk about it first."

"Agreed," Godfrey said through his teeth.

"This is a team effort," Rosa went on. "We need to act like a team. And as the producer, I need to give final approval for everything on the business end. Documents, hiring decisions, everything."

Izzy looked down. So did Godfrey. So did Brewster. Rosa's height automatically gave her a certain authority. But it was her voice, too. It sounded, for lack of a better word, adult.

"I'm sorry," Izzy whispered. "I'm just excited."

"Me too," Brewster said.

"Ditto," Godfrey said.

"That's okay," Rosa said. "Obviously we're all excited."

And she motioned with her chin to Harriet, who was doing an awkward little dance at the helm of the pirate ship, bobbing her shoulders and twirling her fingers and softly singing, "Movie makin', movie makin', gonna do some movie makin'."

It was undeniably charming. And everyone resisted the urge to remind her that it was only a trailer.

Chapter 18

Lights, Camera . . . Inaction!

They all let their parents know that they wouldn't be home for dinner, and they rode the bus together. Carly, however, sat by herself in the back, fiddling with the camera. Godfrey whispered again that she was "most definitely a diva," and no one came to her defense. It was becoming more apparent that he was probably right.

Godfrey got off one stop early so he could collect the makeup and costumes at his house. The rest of them got off at Brewster's stop and walked to the barn. When Carly had caught up, she handed the camera to Brewster. "Here you go, Christopher Nolan."

He examined it carefully, then nodded to Rosa. Everything was intact.

"I'll get my tripod," he said, and headed to his room. When

he got there, he noticed the dyed sheet that he used as a green screen was crumpled up in the corner, so he grabbed that too. Passing his mom on the stairs, he told her, "We're filming today, so that means no distractions."

"Oh, but I was going to invite the girls over for a Zumba class in the backyard," she said.

He knew she was joking, but it didn't make it any less embarrassing. "Seriously, Mom. This is a big deal for us."

"I get it," she said. "And I'll make sure Jade gets it too. Have fun, okay?"

Fun? Work was more like it. But Brewster simply thanked his mom and headed for the door.

By the time he was back in the yard, he found that Harriet was standing inside the hole with a tape measure, Izzy was on the phone with her brother saying, "As many as you can carry," Rosa was rereading the script with a pen in her hand, and Carly was lounging on a chair on the patio, munching on Tostitos and salsa she had obviously taken from Brewster's kitchen.

"We need a whole table of snacks," she said. "Snacks as far as the eye can see."

"Craft services," Izzy told her as she pocketed her phone and pulled out her iPad. "That's what it's called."

"We need that," Carly said.

"We'll check the budget," Rosa said. "But right now, we need to start shooting."

Brewster was already one step ahead of her. He opened the tripod and placed it in the same spot he had placed it when he was filming Carly a few days before. As he attached the camera and checked the shot through the viewfinder, Harriet tapped him on the shoulder.

"Yes?" he said, not turning around.

"You have a green screen!"

"A green sheet, yes," he said, making small adjustments to the angle and the height of the shot.

"Check it out," Harriet said. "I'm invisible!"

Reluctantly, Brewster turned around to find that Harriet had draped the green sheet over her body. She was like a ghost, hopping and twirling and having a grand old time.

"What's with the sheet?" Carly asked as she wiped salsa off her mouth with her sleeve.

"It's the green screen I was telling you about," Brewster said. "Remember?"

Carly shrugged. "You say a lot of things I end up forgetting."

Harriet tossed the sheet off and explained. "It's totally amazing. If you use a background or even clothes that are a weird shade of green like this, then it's super easy to make those things disappear using certain apps. Because all you have to do is say, 'Hey, app! Make all this weird green color disappear!' and *zzzzzap*, it's gone. Then you can put in backgrounds or digital characters wherever the weird green was."

"Could you make someone's head disappear?" Carly asked.

"If you wrapped it in green fabric, you could!" Harriet said.

"Epic," Carly whispered with a nod.

"And we can make this hole disappear," Harriet said as she covered it with the sheet.

"But . . . but . . . but . . . that'll get it dirty," Brewster said.

"That's what washing machines are for," Izzy remarked as she looked up from her iPad. "Plus, it'll keep Carly's clothes from getting dirty."

Two very good points. And seeing the sheet over the hole, Brewster wondered why he hadn't thought of this himself. Precise camera angles and lighting weren't as necessary if Harriet could use the green screen to turn this into a bottomless pit later.

"Fine," he said. "Keep it there."

"Are we happy with Carly's wardrobe?" Rosa asked. "Is it . . . enough?"

Carly looked down at her ensemble, which was what she wore to school that day. A faded yellow concert T-shirt with a woman's face and the word *DRAMARAMA* on it, a frilly blue skirt, and striped white and purple leggings. "Enough of what? Enough Vermont for you? Too much Jersey for your tastes?"

"It's not that," Rosa said. "I mean, does it look good enough?"

"I think she looks great!" Harriet said. "Very retro."

"I like it too," Izzy said. "But I also like that galaxy dress I chose for her."

Rosa didn't seem to care about the other girls' assessments. She turned to Brewster. "Thoughts?"

"Let me see it in front of the camera," Brewster said, pointing to a spot near the hole.

"If you must," Carly said as she munched on one more chip. Then she hopped up from her chair and over to the grass. As she twirled in place, the colors seemed especially vibrant.

"So?" Rosa asked again.

"She looks like herself," Brewster said.

"Which means?" Rosa said.

Brewster didn't think he needed to elaborate, but he did. "She looks great."

Carly did a little curtsy. "Naturally."

"So what are we waiting for?" Brewster asked. "Let's shoot."

This brought a smile to everyone's faces. Yes, they had filmed some footage already, but that didn't feel official. This, on the other hand, did, and it was getting more official by the moment.

"Wait, one more thing!" Izzy cried as she reached into her backpack and pulled out a flat black piece of cardboard. A stack of white paper was stapled horizontally across the front of it, and at the top there was an extra piece, a black-and-white-striped arm that could be lifted and lowered.

"Cool," Harriet said. "You brought one of those *lights-camera-action* thingies."

This is something Brewster definitely knew about, and he

was happy to share his knowledge. "Oh wow," he said. "Izzy made a clapper board."

"Which is?" Rosa asked.

"You write the scene name, the shot, and the take number on the front," Brewster said. "Then you raise that top part and *clap* it down before the director calls action."

"Why?" Rosa asked. "Superstition?"

"It's so you can keep track of all your shots, and make sure the video and audio tracks line up," Brewster said.

"Plus, it's super fun," Izzy said, opening and closing the top like it was a pelican's beak.

"Okay, then," Rosa said. "Let's try it out."

Izzy pulled a Sharpie from her bag and quickly wrote on the top piece of paper.

SCENE: JUMPING IN HOLE	TAKE: 1
DIRECTOR: BREWSTER	
DATE: 5/14/2019	

At the same time, Brewster placed two small stones on the ground, one where Carly was currently standing and one near the edge of the hole.

"Now, this I remember from when we were shooting before," Carly said. "These are my marks, right? I walk from one to the other?"

"Exactly," Brewster said with a smile.

What was happening? This didn't feel like work. Like his mom told him, he was having fun. Everyone was getting along. Everything was running smoothly. Was this even possible? Was this—

"STOOOOOPPPPP!"

Of course, it wasn't possible.

"STOOOOOPPPPP! DON'T SHOOT!"

The voice was Godfrey's. Costumes erupted from his arms as he careened toward Brewster and the camera.

"Slow down," Rosa said. "You'll get them dirty."

Godfrey immediately handed off half the costumes to Rosa and the other half to Izzy. Then he grabbed Brewster by the shoulders. "This is a disaster," he said.

"Wait, what is?" Brewster said, worried that some unseen danger was lurking above or below or possibly all around them. He had promised to keep everyone safe and now—

"Your shot is backlit," Godfrey said.

"What?"

"That means the sun is behind the shot, which makes everything shadowy and washed out," Godfrey said frantically. "And you should really have something in the foreground to show the depth of the field and—"

"You're not happy with the shot?" Brewster asked. "Is that all this is?"

"But that's what matters, right?" Godfrey said. "How it looks? It needs to look perfect, and sorry, Brewster, but while you may have an eye for some things, you don't have an eye for perfect."

Before Brewster even had a chance to get offended, Godfrey moved the tripod and camera over a few feet, and then he hustled to the barn and found a red Radio Flyer wagon. He rolled it in front of the camera, putting it in the foreground, on the left side of the shot. Through the viewfinder, Carly still appeared in the frame. Hands on hips, she waited for instructions.

"Better," Godfrey said. "But can we get her in nicer clothes?"

"What's wrong with what she's wearing?" Brewster said. "It's authentic."

"Movie stars aren't authentic," Godfrey said. "They surpass authentic."

Carly pointed at him. "I like that. What he said."

"Izzy!" Godfrey shouted. "The silver dress!"

The silver dress certainly surpassed authentic. It glittered in the late-day sun, like it was made of mirrors, or perhaps diamond scales. Izzy held it up, and Carly was drawn into its gravity. She ran a hand across the front and asked, "Is it bulletproof?"

"Not that I'm aware of," Godfrey said. "But it's boring-proof."

"I'll put it on!" Carly announced as she snatched it and raced to the barn to change.

"Really?" Brewster said to Godfrey.

"You have a problem with the costume?"

"She's supposed to be a regular girl who discovers a portal in her yard," Brewster said. "Not some model or something."

"This is a trailer, right?" Godfrey said.

"As I keep reminding everyone," Rosa added.

"And because it's a trailer, we don't know what happens in the real movie before this scene or after this scene," Godfrey said.

"I think the audience can make some guesses," Brewster said.

"I think the audience will like things that look beautiful, and that dress looks beautiful," Godfrey said.

"It does," Rosa said.

"It does," Izzy echoed.

"It does," Harriet confirmed.

It really did.

When Carly walked out of the barn wearing the long silver dress, it was undeniable. The fit, the flow, the sparkle, the elegance: This dress was *it*.

"If I saw that in a trailer, I'd think she's super cool. I'd guess she was on her way to a fancy teenage party or something," Izzy said.

"Or the Nobel Prize ceremony," Harriet said.

"Or that," Izzy said with a shrug.

Brewster had to make a decision. Was this a democracy? Or a dictatorship? Who exactly was calling the shots?

"Where's the dress from the other day?" Brewster asked. "With the stars and comets and stuff."

"Here," Rosa said, holding up the dress that had all the swirling galaxies on it.

"If she's not going to wear her regular clothes, then she should wear that," Brewster said.

"It's not nearly as wonderful, though," Godfrey said.

This was true, but . . .

"It doesn't have to be wonderful," Brewster said. "It has to be right. And I'm sorry, Godfrey, but I'm fine with you giving me advice on the set and about the photography and so on. The shot does look better now. Thank you for that. But you're wrong about the dress. It's a really nice dress, but it's not the dress we need. We're going with the galaxy dress. That's my decision, and it's final."

"Yeah, you see, there's—" Godfrey started to say.

But Rosa cut him off. "Our director has spoken, and we will do as he says." She walked the galaxy dress over to Carly and handed it to her.

Carly grabbed it, somewhat reluctantly, but she grabbed it just the same.

"That's still something she could wear to the Nobel Prize ceremony," Harriet said. "Also, why do people keep talking about a trailer? How can you have a trailer when you don't already have a—"

Chapter 19

Here Goes Nothin'

The camera was in place, with the red Radio Flyer wagon in the foreground and the sun in a position where it wasn't backlighting the shot. The green sheet was draped over the hole. Harriet and Rosa sat in lawn chairs on the patio, where they could view the proceedings. Brewster and Godfrey were positioned behind the camera. Izzy stood in front of the camera holding the clapper board in front of her chest. And Carly, wearing the galaxy dress, was on her mark, a few feet behind Izzy.

"I still have to learn about all the things I'm supposed to say before clapping the clapper," Izzy told them. "But for now, I'll name the shot and tell you to start the camera. Then I'll clap the clapper and Brewster will say 'action' and Carly will go. Sound good?"

"As long as I hear 'action,' then I'm acting," Carly said.

"That's all I care about."

"Works for me as well," Brewster said. "I say we try it."

"Sweet," Izzy said as she lifted the top of the clapper board. "Get ready everyone. Jumping in the Hole scene, take one. Roll camera."

Godfrey tapped the record button on the camera while Izzy clapped down on the top of the clapper board and scurried out of the frame.

"And . . . action!" Brewster shouted.

And . . . Carly acted. She paced to the hole and lingered at the edge for a moment, then she shrugged and jumped in, basically belly flopping onto the sheet.

"Cut!" Brewster shouted, and Carly popped up.

"That was funny," Harriet said, because it was.

"We don't want it to be funny," Brewster said. "Let's do it again. But this time with no shrug and no belly flop. What exactly were you doing, anyway?"

"It's called acting," Carly said. "What exactly were you doing?"

"It's called directing."

"Then direct me. I was acting ambivalent. You know, thinking about mustard, like you told me to a few days ago. Isn't that what you want?"

"Not today," Brewster said. "You need to act curious. Like, 'What the heck is this hole? Where did it come from? Where does it lead to?' And maybe you're a bit scared. But also excited. You're trying something new and mysterious. Think about skydiving. Or scuba diving. Maybe you dip a toe in the hole first, like it's a pool and you're testing the water. And then when you jump in, you gotta be protecting your body. All scrunched up."

"I do all of that in five seconds?" Carly said.

"Try different things," Brewster said. "We'll figure out what works. We can do multiple takes. And don't forget your line."

"What's my line?"

"It's in the script."

"My copy is all the way over there," Carly said, pointing to the patio. "Which is far. Just remind me what is."

"Here goes nothin'," Izzy said.

"Is that the line? Or does that mean we're starting?" Carly asked.

Rosa looked up from her copy of the script and said, "That's the line."

"Got it," Carly said.

"And here goes nothin'," Brewster said, putting his hand up so that everyone would be quiet, which meant they were starting.

Izzy got the cue, raised the clapper on the clapper board, and announced, "Jumping in the Hole scene, take two. Roll camera."

"And . . . action."

• • •

With take 1 recorded, they moved on to . . .

Take 2: Where Carly scratched her chin, bit her thumb, smiled, and said, "Here goes nothin'," before cannonballing into the hole. And . . .

Take 3: When, with hands on hips, Carly stared the hole down, her face going through almost every emotion possible until it settled on determination. That's when she ran, hollered, "Here goes nothin'," and jackknifed in. Next was . . .

Take 4: And this time she whispered things to herself, like she was trying to psych herself up or talk herself out of something, before closing her eyes and running straight into the hole as if it were the ocean, while shouting, "Here goes nothin'." As for . . .

Take 5: It would qualify as a blooper. Some misplaced microphone cords hidden in the grass were to blame for screwing things up. At the beginning of the take, Carly flexed her biceps, which was a bit much. Then she snarled like a tiger, which was also a bit much. Finally, she stomped toward the hole, saying her line through clenched teeth. "Here goes noth—" but before she could finish, her ankle got wrapped up in the cord, she swung around in a circle, and stumbled and tumbled and went head over heels into the Radio Flyer wagon, which rolled toward the hole, and as its wheels got tangled up in the green sheet, it dumped Carly out and the cord yanked the camera and the tripod and sent everything spinning.

Laughs were replaced by gasps as Rosa and Brewster rushed

to make sure the camera was okay and Harriet and Izzy rushed to see if Carly was okay and Godfrey stood still, taking deep breaths, clearly trying to process the fact that his perfect composition had been ruined. Thankfully, every object and every person were fine, and after setting it all back up, they moved on to film . . .

Takes 6 through 25: This was where Carly tried pretty much everything else—hopping and flailing and howling and crashing and crawling and rolling and skipping and *here-goes-nothin'*-ing for hours on end. After each attempt, Brewster would yell "Cut!" and they'd reset the scene, Izzy would rip the top page from the clapper board and fill in a new one, and they'd try again.

They moved the camera for some takes, and for other takes they moved Carly. Adjustments followed by adjustments, variations upon variations. It was entertaining and exhausting for everyone, and they lost track of time. They only realized how late it was when the sun was getting low. Brewster didn't want to stop because this was the golden hour, and the light was as perfect as he'd imagined it would be when he wrote the script.

But it was Izzy's job to keep things moving. "I'm sorry, everyone," she said. "I'm supposed to be keeping us on schedule, but this was too much fun to watch. The call sheet says it's time for dinner, but should we skip it and try to fit the other scenes in?"

"I don't really have any dinner for us," Brewster said. "So I don't think we have a choice."

"Will we have a chance to do the popcorn and all that stuff at my house?" Carly asked.

"Dailies, you mean?" Izzy asked.

Carly nodded enthusiastically.

"I think we'll have to call them weeklies," Rosa said. "We can't shoot in the afternoon and then watch it all too. We'd be up until midnight. We're already running behind."

"About that," Harriet said. "I really should go home. It's a school night, you know."

"Yeah, I probably have to go too," Carly said. "If we're not doing the dailies, then are we still shooting every single day?"

"I mean, yeah, that was the plan," Rosa said.

"I have piano practice tomorrow," Harriet said.

"And I have hip-hop dance on Thursday," Izzy said.

"Not to mention homework, and other family commitments," Godfrey said. "Seems like it's okay to do this occasionally, but—"

"Wait," Rosa said. "Does this mean we can't film again until the weekend?"

"I can film every day," Brewster told her.

Saying it, Brewster realized how sad it sounded. Or maybe it didn't sound sad to the others, but it sounded sad to him. Sure, he had homework, but he didn't have piano, or dance, or "other family commitments." His only commitment was this.

"I can film every day too," Rosa said.

While hearing that did make Brewster feel a little less alone, it didn't necessarily help the situation.

"You two can't do much without us," Carly said, which was hard to dispute.

So Brewster didn't. He simply took a deep breath and said, "Fine. In the meantime, we'll keep working on what we've already shot. I'll send Harriet some of the clips so she can start rendering the special effects."

Harriet responded with two thumbs up.

"And we'll meet every day during recess at the pirate ship," Rosa added. "To assign jobs and create call sheets. We'll make sure that when we're ready to film on the weekend, we don't fall behind again."

"Do we need to film anything else in school?" Carly asked.

"I'm not sure yet," Brewster said.

"While you figure that out, I'll take the camera," Carly said, signaling with two fingers for him to hand it over. "Gotta keep Warburton off our backs."

"Yeah, speaking of—" Rosa started to say, but Carly cut in.

"I'm on top of it," Carly said.

"I'll need to keep the memory card," Brewster said as he removed it and slipped it into his pocket. "For editing purposes."

"I can always find another if I need it," Carly said, and she snatched the camera away.

"Is that it for today?" Izzy asked.

"It is for me, so sayonara, suckers," Carly said, and with the camera strap over her shoulder, she made another of her quick and dramatic exits, sashaying away from the bunch without saying another word.

"Sayonara . . . nice people," Harriet said, and she followed, copying Carly's movements, but not very well.

Izzy and Godfrey gathered up the costumes, found some hooks in the barn to hang them on, and then they were on their way too.

Finally, Rosa sent a text to her mom asking for a ride home. The others were all within walking distance, but Rosa's house was a few miles away. Brewster wasn't sure exactly where it was. All he knew was that it was somewhere deep in the woods, down a private road.

"I'm sorry," Brewster told her as they sat on the edge of his front porch, waiting.

"For what?"

"That we didn't get everything done today."

Rosa shrugged. "You're doing your best."

He wasn't sure if that was a compliment or not, and he didn't ask. Instead, he told her, "We'll make up for it this weekend."

"We better," she responded. "We need to have this finished in exactly two weeks. Tuesday, May 28, the day after Memorial Day."

"Why two weeks?"

Rosa hesitated. "Money like this can't last forever."

It seemed like a reasonable thing to say, though he didn't know why, because he'd never had money like that. "We'll make up for it," he said again.

Then they sat in silence for a while, and Brewster's mind wandered to the many takes they had shot that afternoon. He was truly sorry that they hadn't stayed on schedule, but he was also quite happy with what they had accomplished. He couldn't wait to watch Carly's performance and pick out his favorite moments. For all the countless hours he had spent making videos in the past, this was the first time it felt, for lack of a better word, real. This was the first time it felt like it mattered.

His daydreaming was interrupted by the arrival of a large dark SUV in front of his house.

"Where's the fancy red car?" Brewster asked, referring to the one all the kids at school admired.

"That's one of my dad's," she told him as she hopped up. "This is one of my mom's."

It was if she were discussing outfits, something you could change daily and didn't share. Brewster couldn't even try to relate. He simply said, "Well, this one is really fancy too."

Rosa hurried from the porch to the SUV. She gave a little wave over her shoulder, and Brewster called out, "See you tomorrow," as she opened the passenger side door.

Melodic music poured out from inside, and her mom said something, though Brewster couldn't make out the words.

The only thing he could decipher was part of Rosa's annoyed response, which was, "No, Mom, not a boyfriend."

Hearing those words didn't hurt Brewster's feelings. Not even a bit. Girlfriends weren't something he thought much about. But as the SUV roared away into the evening, he still wanted nothing more than to make Rosa proud. By the sounds of it, he had only two weeks to do it.

Chapter 20

Dad Being Dad

Brewster spent a few minutes watching the sunset and thought about how best to shoot the reds and oranges and purples that hugged the mountains. He'd make sure to ask Izzy to put at least one sunset on the schedule.

Once the dark finally started to descend, he cleaned up what was left from the day's shoot, folded the green sheet and the tripod, and tucked them under his arm. When he brought them inside, he found his mom and Jade in the kitchen, sitting together at the breakfast bar, eating sandwiches for dinner.

"Hey, kid," his mom said. "Have a seat."

It was an unusual request, but he had no reason to deny it. He set the equipment down near the stairs and climbed onto a stool next to Jade and his mom. His Subway sandwich was waiting for him there, so he started to unwrap it.

"What's up?" he asked.

"It's about your dad," his mom said.

Brewster's mind immediately went to the text from Saturday night. The one his dad had mistakenly sent him, the one with the picture of some woman named Laura. Even though he had deleted the pic from his phone, it was basically impossible to erase the image from his head. It kept invading his thoughts, in different, mutating versions.

The kiss on the cheek . . . How close to the lips was it? How close to the neck? It changed every time he remembered it. And what about the expression on his dad's face? Joy? Embarrassment? That changed too. His dad hadn't contacted him since, so maybe there was nothing to cover up. Or maybe that was his dad's tricky way of making something that was unseemly seem mundane. Of course, Brewster couldn't help but think that this was what his mom wanted to talk about. Because it couldn't possibly be something worse, could it?

"Is Dad . . . okay?" Brewster asked.

"He's fine," Jade said. "He's Dad being Dad."

"He's taking some time to himself," Brewster's mom said.

"What does that mean?"

"He's staying in Portland for a while," his mom said. "He can work remotely from there as well as he can from here, so he's giving it a try."

For a moment, Brewster's brain went back to Carly's place—

the town house on the hill, with the tiny mailbox and the room that was many rooms and the shirtless stepdad named Ken. Brewster had never thought it was appropriate to ask, but he had been wondering why Carly's dad and mom had split up. Hearing her describe him, Carly's dad sounded like a bit of a jerk, but was that the only reason her parents weren't still together? Or had her mom left him so she could be with Ken instead? And was her dad still in New Jersey, in some regular house where Carly grew up?

Brewster knew his situation was different, but perhaps it wasn't as different as he thought. And he was tempted to ask his mom who his dad was staying with, and if she was okay with the arrangement. He thought of asking her if this was a temporary thing or a permanent thing. He considered any number of questions, but he wasn't sure he wanted answers to any number of questions. He wanted his life to be as it always was, without distractions, so he could focus exclusively on the trailer.

So all he said was, "Will that make Dad happy?"

"It might," his mom told him. "We'll see."

Jade let out a long sigh, then wrapped up their half-eaten sandwich. Climbing down from the stool, they said, "This family is so . . . this family."

Brewster's mom shrugged, but not in a puzzled way. In a way that meant she knew what Jade was talking about, but there was nothing she could do about it. Brewster, on the other hand, wasn't sure what Jade was talking about. His family was different. He was aware of that. But wasn't every family different? Like every person was different? And why would any one difference be any better or worse than any other? As long as no one was getting hurt, what did it matter?

Or was someone getting hurt? Brewster knew that no one was getting hurt physically, but what about emotionally? That was the big question, wasn't it? Brewster was definitely confused and even a little worried, but he wouldn't classify that as suffering. His mom and Jade didn't appear to be suffering either—they'd been acting like they always acted—so maybe he didn't need to worry. Still, something felt off.

"If you want to talk about it," his mom said, "we can talk about it."

"No thanks," Brewster said.

"Maybe later, then."

Maybe in two weeks, he thought. That was Rosa's deadline, and he knew his mind shouldn't be elsewhere if he wanted to finish the job and finish it right. Though now that he had a deadline, he also had to wonder: *What comes next?*

The plan had always been to post the trailer on YouTube, wait for it to go viral, rack up those million views, and then start fielding offers from Hollywood to turn *Carly Lee and the Land of Shadows* into an actual movie. That would remain the plan. But perhaps something else needed to happen first.

Godfrey and Izzy owned a projector and, presumably, a movie screen. Brewster had a barn and plenty of space to entertain guests. And Rosa? Well, Rosa had money.

What if, instead of posting it to YouTube, they held a premiere first? Not virtual. A real-life, face-to-face, dress-up-fancy premiere. They could invite—

"Will Dad be home for Memorial Day weekend?" Brewster asked his mom.

"I don't know," she replied. "You could check with him. Why?"

"We're gonna have a premiere of our trailer. Here. On Memorial Day. Maybe he'd want to come home to attend."

"You finished it?"

"Not quite, but we should be done by then," he said. "Which means I have to get back to work on it."

"You're like a real live adult, aren't you, Brew?" his mom said, which was something she'd been saying for years. Only this time, as he wrapped up his sandwich and headed out of the kitchen, Brewster was really starting to feel like one, with responsibilities and leadership and all the stress that went along with such things.

He returned to his room, and he loaded the memory card into a reader that he plugged into his MacBook. Before uploading the clips to iMovie, he marked them as shareable in his Google Drive so that Harriet could access them. He also added some of the clips from the previous day. Then he sent her a message.

> you can work on the ink stain or the lava or the hole—make sure to look at the script to see how i describe them

The message was on its way before he remembered to add something to it.

> we don't have a lot of time so go as fast as you can

He sent this message before realizing he should send one more.

> but make sure it's top quality like the pros would do

That felt like enough, and he was about to start reviewing the day's footage when he realized he should probably send another final message.

> and thank you

Yes, it was a tacked-on sentiment, but it was the type of thing that adults did, and he was happy with himself for remembering it. Because he knew how good it felt when Rosa recognized his hard work. He made a note to himself in his head:

Make sure to be more appreciative of people.

And as he checked the clock—8:15—he made another note to himself:

And make sure to get at least a little sleep.

Chapter 21

A Grunt for Grunt Work

The rest of the week moved both fast and slow. At school, Brewster went through the motions, doing what he had to do in class, but his mind was always on the trailer. Recess could never come early enough.

They met each day at the pirate ship, where they mapped out the weekend's plans. Carly didn't join them, but they would see her on the playground, often over in the corner near the swings, pointing the movie camera at various kids. She was probably doing nothing worse than filming videos for her TikTok channel, but it still worried Brewster. And it worried him even more when Mr. Warburton asked him to stay after class on Thursday.

"So how are things progressing with the documentary?" Mr. Warburton asked.

Again, lying was nearly impossible for Brewster. Though he

did have the ability to say the bare minimum. "As far as I know, it's going okay."

Mr. Warburton considered this for a few moments and then said, "Carly told me yesterday that it was going great. 'Fantabulous,' she said. But I know she's prone to exaggeration."

"True," Brewster said. "But she's taken the lead on the project, so she knows more about it than I do at this point."

Again. Not a lie. The bare minimum.

"I see," Mr. Warburton said. "You do need a confident director steering the ship. And she's certainly that."

"She certainly is," Brewster said, wondering if he would ever be as confident as Carly. So what Mr. Warburton said next came as a shock.

"You're similar, you know."

Brewster had to confirm what he meant. "Me and Carly?"

"Indeed," Mr. Warburton said. "So I'll tell you what I told her. You both have drive. Passion. That's a good thing. Harness that. It'll get you far. But make sure it doesn't lead you away from being your true self. Don't ignore the things that truly matter."

Brewster wasn't sure what he meant by that. At the moment, getting out of that room and getting back to work were the things that truly mattered to Brewster. So his only reply was, "Yessir, thank you."

This seemed to satisfy Mr. Warburton, and he sent Brewster along to his next class. The knot in Brewster's chest loosened, but not entirely. He knew that they'd have to come clean at some point. When he told Rosa about the meeting, she said she trusted Carly to maintain the charade as long as they needed. "Tricking people makes her happy. Let's keep our star happy."

And so they kept Carly happy by letting her wander around the playground with the camera, while the rest of them discussed sets and lighting and costumes. By Friday, they figured out that there was a ridiculous number of responsibilities to share, and they needed to clearly designate who was doing what.

"I'm not fetching costumes anymore," Godfrey said. "I am not a common mule."

"And I can't spend my extra time preparing snacks and meals when I should be focusing on direction and editing," Brewster added.

"I know no one has asked me to lift heavy things yet, but if they do, I'm not going to lift heavy things," Harriet said. "In case you haven't noticed, I'm not a strong person."

Which led to a realization.

"We need a PA," Izzy said.

"What's that?" Rosa asked.

"A production assistant," Izzy said. "No one here wants to fetch things or move things. We all want to focus on what we're good at. We need someone for grunt work."

Suddenly there was a sound from under the pirate ship. Someone coughing, or maybe choking. Perhaps grunting. But when Brewster looked down through the cracks in the deck boards, he didn't see someone who was sick or hurt. What he saw was Liam Wentworth. Smiling up at him. Waving. And then stepping out through an opening below the deck and revealing himself with an enthusiastic display of jazz hands.

"Heeeere's Liam!" he said with gusto.

They all stared at him blankly.

"It's from a movie," he explained. "And a TV talk show."

Brewster had no idea what he was referring to.

"Sorry," Liam said. "My name is Liam Wentworth."

"We know who you are, Liam," Rosa said, because everyone did. Liam wasn't quite infamous or notorious, but he had his reputation. For sticking his nose in things and always being there when you didn't want him there. Brewster wasn't the only person who tried to avoid him.

"We simply want to know what on earth it is that you want," Godfrey said.

"I've been sitting below deck, and I couldn't help but hear that you've all been working on one of Brewster's videos," Liam said.

"It's a trailer, actually," Harriet said. "For a movie that doesn't exist."

"That makes perfect sense," Liam said. "And it sounds wonderful. I'd love to be involved in some way. I'll be the grunt you need. I love being a grunt."

Liam was the definition of a kiss-up or a yes-man, the sort of person who would agree with anything you said. Most of the time, it was annoying, but now . . .

"So you want to be a . . . What do you call it, Izzy?" Rosa asked.

"Production assistant," Izzy said.

"One of those?" Rosa asked.

Liam nodded.

Brewster was about to object, because the thought of spending more time with Liam was even less appealing than spending more time with Godfrey. But, like Godfrey, Liam had something they needed. So Brewster kept quiet for the moment and let the others take the lead.

"We'll have to interview you first," Rosa told Liam.

"I'd like that," he said.

Godfrey started the process. "Would you be willing to carry costumes for us?"

Liam nodded.

"Lift things that are very heavy and carry them from one place to another place?" Harriet asked.

Another nod.

"Did I say that they were heavy?" Harriet added.

Nod.

"Would you do whatever we tell you to do, whenever we tell you to do it, for however long it takes, even if it means you don't have any time for TV or video games or cons?" Izzy asked.

The nods kept coming.

"And can you start this very second?" Izzy added.

Before he could nod again, Rosa put up a hand and said, "I'm sick of people making decisions without my approval. I'm the producer here, so I'll do the hiring."

"Oh yeah," Izzy said. "Sorry."

Rosa turned to Liam and asked, "Can you start this very second?"

And . . . he shook his head.

"Why not?" they all asked at the same time.

"Because the bell is about to ring, and we have to get to Warburton's class, and I don't want you to get in trouble again for filming in his class, so I figure it would be better for me to start after class if that's okay with everyone."

It was. And that's how the team became a lucky seven.

Chapter 22

Time Travel Machines

Brewster planned to take Friday night off. Or at least he told himself he wouldn't stare at the screen of his MacBook and re-edit the footage one more time. Instead, he was going to stare at the screen of his TV and learn from his dad's movie collection.

James Bond. Indiana Jones. Mad Max. Classic action heroes.

Carly Lee and the Land of Shadows was supposed to be a fantasy film, but since the other kids were handling the costumes, sets, and special effects, Brewster thought it was best for him to focus on how to shoot action. The trailer was bursting with it, after all. So he popped in the Blu-rays, skipped over the dialogue scenes, and focused on the fun stuff.

James Bond running from a villain and leaping from a plane.

Indiana Jones running from a boulder and leaping from a horse.

Mad Max running from a moving car and leaping from . . . another moving car.

The one thing Brewster consistently noticed was how many of the stunts were shot at a distance. Like Carly on the monkey bars, this was a good indicator of an effective action sequence because the audience could always tell what was happening. Plus, the camera didn't bounce around. The editing was fluid. The effects seemed natural. There was a lot to take in with each movie, and Brewster watched the sequences over and over again until . . .

He fell asleep on the couch.

Long nights and school had dealt their blows, and Brewster's body threw in the towel. At some point someone, either his mom or Jade, made sure he was comfortable, because when he woke, he was cuddled up with a blanket and pillow. He wasn't feeling particularly cozy, though. A startling sound had woken him, and it made his body bolt upright.

Bam!

A door had slammed shut. The sound didn't come from the TV, which was now off. It came from outside.

Brewster crept cautiously to the window to investigate. Nudging the curtain back an inch was enough for him to spot his neighbor Piper Barnes sitting on her front steps, with her elbows on her knees and her head in her hands. She was hugged by the glow of a streetlight above her. From inside her house came an angry voice, though Brewster couldn't hear what it was saying. He could only hear Piper's response.

Without raising her head, she yelled back, "Go away. I hate you. I've always hated you."

The words were so sharp. So harsh. So mean. They weren't swears, but they felt like swears. And yet, Brewster could hear the pain in Piper's voice. He couldn't relate—no one in his family ever spoke like that—but he also couldn't help but feel bad for her.

For a minute or two he watched, waiting to see if anyone would come out to talk to her. No one did. At a certain point, she raised her head and took some deep breaths, like she was trying to collect herself. She didn't stand up, though. Instead, she looked up. Perhaps at the stars.

Brewster loved looking at the stars. He loved thinking about how the universe was filled with billions of galaxies, each containing billions of stars, and how each of those stars might have, on average, one planet orbiting it. A billion times a billion worlds. A billion squared. For some people, the vastness of space made them feel insignificant. But for Brewster, it made him feel the opposite. When he looked at the stars, it made him feel like anything was possible.

That feeling was something he hoped Piper could feel too. He didn't know what was going on with her, but he figured that a feeling like that couldn't hurt. So rather than close the curtain and pretend he didn't see her, like part of him wanted to do, he walked over to the front door, opened it, and stepped out onto his front porch.

She noticed and stood. The two of them locked eyes for a moment.

"Hey," she said, then she wiped a tear from her face and bowed her head.

"Hey."

"It's late. You should be in bed."

"I couldn't sleep."

Piper thought for a moment about what she was going to say and settled on, "Neither could I."

Brewster pointed up at the stars and said, "They're pretty tonight."

"Yeah," she said, and she finally looked back up at him. "Do you know the constellations?"

"Only the Big Dipper."

"Me too."

"But sometimes I think about how, if my eyes were strong enough, I could see the edge of the universe and then I'd understand so much more because I'd be looking at the beginning of everything. At the Big Bang."

"Really? How does that work?"

"It has something to do with light and how fast it travels, so when you're looking at stars, you're really looking back in time.

Which means the farther you look, the farther back in time you're seeing."

This made Piper smile. "Like a time machine?"

"Or a movie," Brewster said. "You know, old movies were done on film, and film is just light captured on celluloid."

"Celluloid? Is that, like, fat?"

"No, it's like strips of film. It's black, but also clear. I don't fully understand it, but I know it captures light. The light is actually absorbed onto the film. So when you watch an old movie, you're really looking at light from a long time ago. You're looking back in time."

"That's cool," Piper said.

Brewster wasn't sure if he should say what he said next, but he said it anyway. "Do you need somewhere to sleep tonight?"

"What do you mean?"

"I don't know. Forget it. It's . . . If there was a problem with your . . . room. We have a guest room and—"

"I'll be okay," Piper said with a little sniffle. "Thanks anyway. I might go inside and watch a movie. See if the light from the past looks better than the light from today."

To Brewster, it usually did. But he didn't tell her that because he didn't want to depress her. Instead, he said, "That sounds like a good idea. I'll be seeing ya."

"I'll be seeing ya, too."

With that, they both returned to their houses.

Tomorrow was a big day. The biggest yet. Brewster needed more sleep. So he brushed his teeth and headed for his room. But before he dozed off again, he took one last look out the window, one last chance to ponder the light from the stars.

Chapter 23

Storyboardin'

It was barely past dawn, and Brewster was in the barn, setting things up for the day's shoot, when he heard a gentle knock. He slid the doors open to find Harriet standing in the yard, hands in pockets, sketchbook tucked under an arm.

"You're early," he said.

"I'm worried," she replied.

"About what?"

"That I'm not doing enough."

Brewster was tempted to agree. After all, Harriet had supposedly been working on some special effects and had nothing to show for it. He didn't want to seem mean, but he needed an update. So he asked, "Is this about the lava and all that stuff? I know that special effects are hard, but it *is* your job."

"Oh, that's basically done," Harriet said with a dismissive

wave. "I'm talking about helping you get ready for today. Can we sit down?"

"Sure," Brewster said, dropping an extension cord and pointing to some camping chairs that had strips of white tape stuck on the back of them. Names of individual cast and crew members were written in black marker on the tape.

When Harriet spotted her chair, her body trembled with excitement. "Oh, my goodness. That's my name!"

"Yep, and this one is mine," Brewster said as he grabbed the nicest of the chairs and set it in front of a table. "Did you want to show me what you've been working on?"

"I can show you later," Harriet said as she pulled her chair up to the table. "I wanted to show you this."

She laid her notebook on the table and opened it, revealing what looked like the template for a comic book or graphic novel. White boxes with black frames filled the pages, but there were no images in them. They were empty. It didn't exactly thrill Brewster to see what amounted to a whole bunch of nothing.

"And this is . . . ?"

"Storyboards," Harriet said. "I thought it might help today. You tell me how you imagine the trailer will look, and I'll draw it. That way, when it's time to turn on your camera, you can look at this and see if it matches."

"You can do that?"

Harriet shrugged. "I can try."

Brewster grabbed his copy of the script and flattened it on the table next to the notebook. "Can you draw this?" he asked, pointing to the first scene in the script.

INT. CARLY'S BEDROOM—MORNING

`A cool room, with lots of cool stuff in it.`

"What kind of cool room?" Harriet asked. "And what kind of cool stuff?"

The description was admittedly vague. But Brewster did have a clear idea of what he wanted.

"Action figures. Old collectibles. Electronics. On shelves and in displays. Like a museum or a store." As he said it, he realized he was describing Godfrey and Izzy's room. Or maybe a curiosity shop.

That's basically what Harriet sketched in the first box. Roughly and in pencil, but the shapes and proportions were correct. She was a friend of Izzy's, so it was likely that she'd been in their room. But it was still impressive that she was re-creating this from memory.

"Good," Brewster said. "Really good. Why don't we try the next part?"

`Gorgeous light breaks through an open window. A breeze blows the curtains.`

"Is it a shaft of light or a burst?" Harriet asked.

"A shaft."

"What are the curtains like?"

"Thin. White. Wavy. With star designs on them." This was what the curtains looked like in Jade's room, but he knew he could film some cutaway shots there and then splice them in with the footage of Godfrey and Izzy's room and the audience wouldn't know it was two different places.

Harriet sketched out the curtains and window in the next box.

"Really nice," Brewster said. "You're good at this."

Harriet twirled her pencil in her fingers and said, "It's my superpower. Like you with directing movies."

It wasn't the first time Brewster had been complimented like this—Liam had complimented him plenty—but it felt different coming from someone who was so artistically talented. It felt like true validation. Winner winner chicken dinner.

"Thanks," Brewster said. "Let's try some more."

Harriet's pencil moved quickly, and so did Brewster's mouth, as they went through the script moment by moment, shot by shot, detail by detail. Within an hour they had a good chunk of the script storyboarded.

The day's call sheet showed Liam arriving at 7:30 a.m. He was there by 7:12 a.m., peeking in through the barn doors and saying, "Liam Wentworth, reporting for duty."

There were plenty of things for Liam to do, but for the

moment Brewster was focused on the storyboards. "Here," he said, handing over Harriet's sketchbook. "Scan this or take a photo of it or whatever. Make sure everyone has a copy."

"Aye aye, Cap'n," Liam said, saluting Brewster and then grabbing the sketchbook and disappearing from the barn.

It was annoying, but it was also helpful.

For the next few minutes, Brewster and Harriet discussed what they needed to do to set up any shots that required special effects. She thought of problems and solutions that he never would've, and vice versa. They made a fantastic team.

Before long, the rest of the team arrived.

First it was Rosa, who brought a bag full of extra equipment—new lights, cords, and microphones. She announced that the meals would be catered by the local restaurant, Pizza Nirvana. It was an inspired choice.

Next came Izzy and Godfrey, whose parents drove them in a loud and rusty van laden with costumes and props.

Then there was Carly, who seemed happy, well rested, and ready to work, to everyone's relief.

Finally, Liam returned, breathless and sweaty, holding printed copies of the storyboards, as well as a poster-size version. "Don't ask me how I got it so fast," he said.

They didn't. They simply appreciated his dedication to the job.

Breezy and warm, with a sky full of clouds that were full of personality, the day was perfectly pleasant, which was reflected in everyone's mood as they set up the first shot. The call sheet showed that shooting would begin at 9:30. At 9:25, they were all in their places. For once, everyone was ready.

Chapter 24

Cue the Montage

Carly Meets Palivar, Take 4: Filmed in a dark corner of the barn, the best take of the bunch featured Godfrey in full evil mode, cackling and twirling in his flowing robe. It was also a showcase for Carly's best acting. She looked fierce and brave and scared and worried all at once. Plus, there was smoke! Not from a smoke machine, which they couldn't afford, but from humidifiers duct-taped to vacuum hoses. When positioned near the camera lens, they created the effect of a hazy, smoky filter. It was Rosa's idea. As a frequent sufferer of sinus infections, she was well acquainted with puffs of mist filling her room.

The Sprite: Izzy appeared in multiple scenes as a magical character known as the Sprite. She didn't speak much—mostly climbing trees, hopping around, and pointing enthusiastically—but she had to remain in her makeup and costume all day.

Therefore, it was both disconcerting and hilarious to see a pointy-eared, winged fairylike creature running around set keeping everything on schedule. "Places, people! We're making a masterpiece here today!" she shouted as she pulled up her fern-covered tights and adjusted her crown of daisies.

Craft Services: The delivery woman from Pizza Nirvana couldn't have arrived too soon. It was only 10:30 a.m., but the kids were already starving. Pizzas, salads, sandwiches, mozzarella sticks, the works. She laid it all out on a card table Brewster had dragged to a shady part of the lawn.

"What should I do with all the pasta?" she asked Rosa.

"That's for dinner," Rosa said. "Is there room in the fridge, Brewster?"

"There's always room in the fridge," Brewster replied, because his family rarely cooked.

"There's never room in my fridge," Liam said. "We always have too much chili. So, so much chili."

"We have kale. And kombucha!" Harriet said, with more spirit behind the word *kombucha* than Brewster had ever heard.

"We have three fridges," Godfrey said. "One for fruits and veggies, one for meats and dairy, and one for biodegradable costumes."

"What's a biodegradable costume?" Harriet asked.

"Spaghetti wigs," Izzy said. "Radish necklaces. Cabbage vests."

"Cabbage vests?" Liam said.

Izzy unbuttoned the green fuzzy coat she was wearing as part of her costume and revealed a vest underneath that was made of purple cabbage leaves sewn together. "Cabbage vests," she said.

Mrs. Boddington's Garden: There was no cabbage in Mrs. Boddington's garden, only flowers. But the neighbor's yard was the perfect spot to film what was bound to be a highlight of the trailer. The moment took place amid tulips and daffodils, and it would require special effects.

In terms of the story of the film, Carly travels back and forth through the portal between the real world and the Land of Shadows, but she can never truly escape the Land of Shadows. The inky blackness that covered the whiteboard in the school scene was evidence of it creeping into her regular existence.

And something similar would happen in this scene. The idea was that Carly would walk through the flowers, and as she passed, the flowers would either turn black, or possibly wilt, depending on how good Harriet was at special effects. Brewster still trusted Harriet with the special effects—thanks to her impeccable drawing skills—but having not seen any of those special effects, he wasn't sure how much to trust her.

"Do we need to spray-paint all the flowers neon green?" Brewster asked. "You know, so you can change them in post?"

"Do you think Mrs. Boddington would like that?" Rosa asked.

"Do you think Mrs. Boddington's bodyguards would like that?" Carly added.

Mrs. Boddington's German shepherds, Wilhelm and Wolfgang, were watching them from a back window of the house, their mouths gnawing on bully sticks that Rosa had brought to keep them from going after the cast and crew. They had already chewed halfway through their treats and, with saliva dripping down their chins, appeared to be deciding what to chew on next. The only thing standing between the dogs and the kids was a thin window screen.

"Don't worry about any paint," Harriet said, trying not to make eye contact with the dogs. "I can make it work."

"Yeah," Brewster said nervously. "We should probably get the shot and move along."

The pooches licked their lips.

Social Media Blackout: At a certain point, Brewster had to make an executive decision and confiscate all the phones on set. Izzy seemed to be taking a lot of pics, and Carly would occasionally sneak off with her iPhone camera set on selfie mode to record something in secret. He couldn't have any of that.

"This is a closed set," he told them. "You can't be posting anything on Instagram or TikTok that might take away from the magic of what we're creating."

"Are you afraid my posts will get more likes than the trailer?" Carly asked.

He hadn't been afraid of that. Until she said it! But he was mostly afraid of something else. "If you're distracted by *that*, then you won't be fully invested in *this*," he told them. "The trailer will suffer."

"What about building buzz?" Izzy asked.

"There's a beehive over in the crab apple tree if you want buzz," he said, and he shook a little plastic sand bucket in front of everyone.

Reluctantly, they added their phones. And he kept the bucket by his side all day, which kept the kids honest.

Know what? Brewster was right. With fewer distractions, everything improved. The shoot went smoother and quicker. The cast and crew seemed happier. And no one else in the world got a look behind the curtain.

Brewster knew that the element of surprise was essential for any trailer. That's how you got the big wows. Big wows were impossible if you treated the audience to little wows in advance.

The Wentworth Advantage: Liam Wentworth may have been a bit annoying, but he was entirely essential. Somehow, whenever and wherever he was needed, he was there, and he was willing to do . . . almost anything.

"Carry this bucket of dirt, Liam."

"Happily!"

"Dump the bucket of dirt on the ground, Liam."

"You bet I will!"

"Put on that costume and then roll in the dirt and get the costume so dirty that it looks like it's been through years of sorrow and strife, Liam."

"I would like nothing better!"

He didn't always do the best job. He dropped things, such as a light that shattered all over Godfrey and Izzy's room. He misunderstood instructions, like when Brewster asked him to go fetch a new memory card—the type you put in a camera and record videos on—and instead he brought Brewster a deck of Concentration cards—the kids' game where you must memorize images on cards that are flipped over. And he didn't smell particularly good. But you couldn't really fault him for that. He was working hard, and sweating because of it, and smiling the whole time.

Action, Action, Action: A good chunk of the day was spent on choreographing and filming a ten-second action sequence that was supposed to be the centerpiece of the trailer. In it, Carly had to sprint through a dark cave, then throw punches and swing roundhouse kicks at flying creatures that would explode into glittery bursts of light.

Rather than rely on CGI, both Brewster and Harriet thought it would be better to go with practical effects. To that end, they created creatures from thin black balloons filled with silver glitter and helium, a tank of which the Tarkingtons had somehow acquired. It was no surprise that Godfrey knew a bit of balloon artistry and could twist the rubber into insect-like creatures that they referred to as Shadowzoids. To make them pop, it was as simple as attaching pins to the tips of Carly's shoes and her fingernails. When Carly made a direct hit, the creature would burst and the glitter would fly and, hopefully, catch the light, causing it to shimmer in the darkness.

Since Brewster wanted the sequence to compete with the great sequences he'd watched the night before, he thought it would be cool to film it all in one shot, from a distance, with Carly fighting and running and jumping. That required planning, and patience, and take after take after take. They went through countless balloons and bags of glitter, but thanks to everyone's hard work, they managed to pull off a single take where the balloons entered the frame at the right moments and Carly hit and popped every one of them and looked somewhat good doing it. It would have to suffice.

The Golden Hour: The day finished with a shot at the local park, where the sun was hanging low over the Green Mountains and the dandelions were thick in the soccer field. They had gotten through so many scenes that they had a good chunk of the trailer already shot. This scene wasn't on the call sheet, or in the script, but Brewster thought of it at the last minute.

"Can we get a shot where Carly collapses, like she's just returned home from the Land of Shadows and she's exhausted?" he asked.

"Do I get to lie down?" Carly asked.

"Yep," he said. "That's the point."

"Then count me in," she said, falling back onto a blanket of green and yellow.

They got the shot, and it was a lovely one. Then everyone else plopped down too. They all needed it. For a few quiet moments, they lay there in the grass and flowers and the only sounds were the wind and Liam's snores. It had been a long day.

Finally, Dailies: When filming was wrapped and the sets were cleaned up, they grabbed the pasta from the fridge and headed over to Harriet's house, because she insisted on hosting, and she promised a surprise.

"Is it kom . . . bucha?" Liam asked warily.

"No, but almost as good," Harriet assured him.

Chapter 25

One Condition

Harriet's house was humble. That means it wasn't big and it didn't have a lot of things in it. But it was neat, and warm, and inviting. Exactly like her.

Harriet's parents and little sister were expecting them and had set a table with seven chairs in front of the TV, which was smaller than Carly's TV, but big enough for what they needed.

Harriet introduced her parents and lovingly recounted the story of how they met when her mom was working for the Peace Corps and her dad was a teacher in a small African school, and they got stuck together for a night in a broken-down Jeep at the foot of Mount Kilimanjaro. Her dad, Daniel, was from Tanzania and he spoke with an accent that Brewster would have described as quiet and happy. Harriet's mom, Trish, was from Alabama, and she spoke with an accent that Brewster would have also described as quiet and happy, but a different version of quiet and happy.

Kaia, Harriet's four-year-old sister, wasn't exactly quiet (she was quite loud, in fact), but she was plenty happy. "Let's watch *Paw Patrol*!" she shouted as she hopped up and down in front of the TV.

"No, no, no," Daniel said. "The big kids are watching their movie tonight."

"Mommy and Daddy will play some Candyland with you, 'kay?" Trish said. "Let Harriet and her friends have some time to themselves."

Kaia didn't like this decision at first, until she gave it some thought. "Okay," she said through gritted teeth. "But I'm winning."

"Of course, because you are the very best at Candyland," Daniel told her as he hoisted the little girl up, kissed her on the cheek, and then put her onto his shoulders so he could carry her to the other side of the house.

Meanwhile, Trish had set a tray of food in the middle of the table. "I know y'all have your pasta, but I made a few sides to go with it. Kimchi. Daal. Labneh. All of Harriet's favorites."

"I don't know what any of those things are," Liam said.

"How about popcorn?" Carly asked.

Trish winked and then headed for the kitchen. "I'll see what I can do."

"Thank you, Mrs. Joseph," Liam called out.

"She goes by her maiden name," Harriet told him. "Armstrong."

"Oh no, I'm so sorry," Liam said, and he slapped himself on the hand as punishment. "That was a huge mistake."

"No, it wasn't. Happens all the time. She doesn't mind," Harriet said cheerily, and you could tell she meant it, because she always meant what she said.

Liam's tense body unfurled with relief. But Brewster's body did the opposite. It clenched up with a realization. Brewster's mom also went by her maiden name: Kendall. That wasn't particularly odd. Lots of kids had moms who went by their maiden names. But the difference was, his mom hated being called by his father's last name: Gaines. She always corrected people immediately when they made the mistake. She was "a Kendall and will always be a Kendall," and any other implication made her angry. Not that Brewster wished that his mom would be a Gaines like he was. But at that moment, thinking about his own parents and their decisions, Brewster wondered why he couldn't be a Kendall too.

"I have a surprise for everyone," Harriet announced, stealing Brewster's attention back. "Before we watch what we filmed today, I wanna show you something I've been working on for a while."

She tapped an iPad and a video appeared on the TV screen.

And what a video it was! While it wasn't very long, it was beyond impressive. It started in school with the scene they had filmed guerrilla-style in Mr. Warburton's class. Immediately, Brewster recognized that it was his edit of the scene, but Harriet had done something to the color. It was more vibrant, and more consistent, while Brewster's original version had featured sections that were dull and washed out. She had obviously done something to make all the tints and hues and brightness levels match. In short, it looked good.

Then came the special effect: the expanding black ink blot on the whiteboard. It started as a tiny dot and then quickly bloomed into an amoeba-shaped shadow that swirled and squirmed and expanded. In short, it looked—

"Fantastic!" Izzy shouted when it appeared on-screen. While the blob wasn't very realistic, it was weird and unsettling. Which was fantastic indeed. Exactly what they needed.

"I couldn't fix the sound," Harriet said, when Carly's garbled dialogue played. "I'm not good with sound."

"Don't worry," Brewster said. "We'll rerecord it and dub it over the top."

"Sort of like the opposite of lip-synching, right?" Carly said. "I can do that."

"It's called ADR: Automated Dialogue Replacement," Brewster said, because Izzy wasn't the only one who had been reading up on film terms.

"That sounds like a robot will be doing it," Liam remarked.

"Got that, Rosa?" Carly said. "Put a talking robot in the budget to redo all my lines!"

It got a good laugh from everyone except Rosa. Brewster had noticed she was quieter than normal during the day's shoot, which he had chalked up to her taking things seriously. But dailies were the fun and relaxing part of the day, so he didn't understand why she was still quiet. Then again, he didn't completely understand Rosa.

When the classroom scene was over, the video cut to black and then faded back in on the scene with Carly on the monkey bars. While the first scene was slightly different than the version Brewster had put together, this one was entirely new. Only Carly remained. The entire background was gone, and in its place there was dancing fire, spitting lava, billowing smoke, and—

"O . . . M . . . G," Carly said. "I look even more awesome than I did before."

She truly did. The whole scene did. Again, it wasn't exactly realistic. There was a cartoonishness to it. But a little suspension of disbelief goes a long way, and if Harriet could maintain the same quality of special effects throughout the trailer, it would make this a convincing otherworldly dimension.

"Thank you," Brewster said as soon as the screen went black again.

Harriet clasped her hands together in joy and replied, "You're welcome. My dad helped. He's the one who taught me."

"Thank him too, then," Brewster said. "Thank you to everyone."

This was perhaps the sincerest thanks Brewster had ever given. He truly meant it. And it seemed the others could tell. Godfrey, of all people, smiled back at him and said, "Thank you, too. We seem to be getting things done, don't we?"

To Brewster, that was an understatement. Because seeing what Harriet had created, and knowing everything that they had accomplished that day alone, made him believe that not only could they get things done, but they could get things done right.

He began to picture it. The one. The six zeros. The million views. They felt closer than ever, and imagining the number got his pulse racing and made him forget about any strange feelings or questions he was having about his family.

His excitement couldn't be contained. That's why he blurted out the big plans he'd been considering. "We're having a premiere. Memorial Day. Exactly nine days from now."

"You mean that's when we're posting it on YouTube?" Rosa asked.

"No," Brewster said. "A *real* premiere. Red carpet and everything. Can we make sure we have enough money in the budget to buy a red carpet? I mean, we could hold it at my place. In the yard and in my barn. Which is free. Izzy and Godfrey have a projector and screen. Can we use those?"

"Cool with me," Izzy said, and Godfrey nodded his consent.

"And I have a bunch of chairs," Brewster went on. "We can invite our friends, our family, whoever. All we need is that red carpet. And maybe food."

"I think that's an incredible idea," Carly said. "And I can wear that shimmery dress that Godfrey picked out for me."

"And I can go in character as Palivar!" Godfrey said.

"And I might even be invited!" Liam shouted.

It was sad and cute at the same time, and it made Brewster laugh. "Of course you'll be invited, Liam. You did amazing today. So it's settled, then?"

Carly held up her phone. "Already put it in my calendar."

Again, Rosa was silent, seemingly unmoved by the proposal. Brewster assumed that she would pipe up with some cynicism. "Are you sure this is the best use of our money?" or "Let's focus on finishing the movie first." But she didn't. She simply stared at the TV, which was now off. Perhaps it was best to ask her directly.

"What do you think, Rosa?" Brewster said. "About the premiere?"

It was clear that she was thinking about something. Because it took her a while to respond. And when she did, the first thing she said didn't sound honest.

"I think it sounds really fun," she replied with the enthusiasm one reserves for removing a splinter.

"Does that mean we can buy a red carpet?" he asked.

Rosa nodded, and the next thing she said sounded completely honest. "One condition. My family will not be invited."

Chapter 26

The Snidious Nurk

Brewster's family would be invited. He'd already told his mom, and he planned to tell Jade as soon as he saw them again. At first, he thought of calling his dad, explaining that this was very important to him, and it would mean a lot if he could fly back home to join in the celebration. That was what any kid would do, right?

Yet somehow, it felt like begging. More specifically, it felt like begging to someone who didn't necessarily deserve it. His dad had flown to the other side of the country. He had decided to stay there. For peace and quiet? To be with someone else? Brewster didn't know because his dad hadn't told him. Nothing. Not even a text (unintentional ones not included). Which didn't surprise Brewster. It angered him, however. The more he thought about it, the more it ate at him, and the more it made him ask himself a simple and awful question.

Would his life be better with a different dad?

One who didn't treat him like a roommate. One who was kind and boring and checked in on him. One who had rules about when to adjust the thermostat and who got mildly upset when his son told him that he didn't want to join the soccer team. Or the chess club, for that matter. One who noticed. His dad wasn't a bad person, but to Brewster, he certainly didn't feel like a good dad.

And what about a different mom?

One whose feelings actually got hurt. One who was passionate about the father of her kids, in one way or another. Love or hate. Either would do. Something! One who hugged and kissed her son, and one who didn't always trust her son to make decisions for himself. One who didn't call him an adult. One who called him a kid, because that's what he was. A kid. He was twelve. Twelve!

Of course, replacing his parents would be like replacing his hands or his eyes. They were part of him. He loved and needed them. He just desperately wanted to know them in the ways that Godfrey and Carly and Harriet seemed to know their parents. He wanted his mom and dad to stop everything and focus exclusively on him and what he was doing. Not all the time, but maybe every once in a while. Mostly, he wanted a connection, an assurance that his family was in this together. If only to know what such an experience felt like.

An idea!

Brewster realized the best way to see if this could ever happen would be to see how his father reacted when invited to the premiere. But he knew the invitation had to be as emotionless as possible. So rather than call him or text him a personal message, Brewster decided to send his dad the official invitation, the basic Evite with all the details, the same thing he planned to send to his elementary school friends: Tyler, Henry, Elijah, and Luke. Brewster would make the premiere seem like a big deal—because it was a big deal!—but he wouldn't try to convince his dad either way.

A super-amazing event is happening, and you're invited. Join us before we reach a million views. Or don't. It's your choice.

Or something along those lines.

That way, his dad could decide between supporting his son or focusing on himself, with little to no influence from Brewster. Then Brewster would know exactly where his dad stood. This was especially important, because once the trailer posted and people saw how amazing it was, it would be hard to trust anyone's motives when they treated him well. Once it reached a million views, all bets were off.

With the plan set, Brewster typed up the Evite, chose some graphics, and compiled a small list of his guests (everyone involved in the filming agreed they could each invite up to ten people). Before he went to bed, he sent it off, which felt both exciting and terrifying. The countdown had officially begun.

Presenting . . .
The world premiere of the trailer for . . .

CARLY LEE AND THE LAND OF SHADOWS

Time: Monday, May 27, at 3 PM
Location: Brewster's Barn Theater

Walk the red carpet and be the first of millions to see the newest viral sensation!

• • •

Sunday's schedule was full. But they had storyboards and a tight script. They had the Tarkingtons' van full of costumes and props. They had craft services—burgers, mac and cheese, and other comfort food provided by a local food truck called Mmm Mmm Mmm. They had a cast and crew that was ready to go, and they started early and went late.

Along with the call sheet, they constructed a more in-depth shot list that featured wide shots (lots of stuff in the frame), medium shots (some stuff in the frame), and close-up shots (faces and hands and little stuff in the frame). They also noted tracking shots (moving), zooms (getting bigger or smaller), and POVs (shots from a character's point of view).

It looked like this:

Production:	*Carly Lee and the Land of Shadows*	**Director:** Brewster Gaines		**Date:** May 19, 2019

Shot #	Description	Type of Shot	Location	Cast
1	The Sprite is imprisoned in a "cage of thorns."	Medium	Playground	Izzy, Godfrey
2	The battle rages—Carly and Palivar fight on the "Fields of the Forgotten" as the Sprite struggles to escape from the "cage of thorns."	Wide	Park	Carly, Godfrey, Izzy
3	Carly descends into the murky depths of the "Cave of the Shadowzoids."	POV	Hiking trail near the park	Carly
4	Clouds sweep over the mountains.	Extreme Wide	Skyline as seen from the park	None
5	Carly runs down the street to catch the bus.	POV	Street near Brewster's House	Carly
6	Kids appear worried at Carly's behavior.	Wide	Street near Brewster's House	Liam, Harriet, Brewster
7	Fierce eyes! Ready to kick butt.	Close-Up	Barn	Carly
8	Palivar sneers and grips his scepter.	Zoom	Barn	Godfrey
9	A pale hand grabs Carly's wrist.	Close-Up	Barn	Carly... and Rosa's hand?
10	A Shadowzoid crawls out of the hole.	Medium	The Hole	None

The shots listed (the first ten out of thirty scheduled for the day) weren't filmed in the order they would appear in the trailer. It made more logistical sense to shoot out of order, which was common for most productions. They also didn't represent all the options at a crew's disposal.

There were other ways they could've listed shots, such as one, two, or three shots, depending on how many people were in the frame. There were over-the-shoulder shots (as it sounds) and cowboy shots (not necessarily as it sounds). There were different ways to focus too. There was rack focus, where one character or object goes out of focus while another one comes into focus. There was wide focus, where everything in the frame was in focus. And there was split-diopter focus, where close-up things and faraway things were in focus, but the things in the middle, not so much. Split-diopter focus was rare, and usually for show-offs.

Izzy and Brewster were still learning many of these terms, and probably even using some additional techniques without knowing that they were. But for the purpose of the shot list, they kept things relatively simple. And it kept them moving.

By the end of the day, they had shot everything they had planned to shoot—and then some! They were confident they could easily finish all the principal photography on the following Saturday. But they needed to dedicate that entire day to the hardest action sequence of all. And they needed one thing they didn't currently have: a go-kart.

Not just any go-kart, mind you, and certainly not a borrowed go-kart. They needed one that they could transform into a monster. And then destroy. In fact, they were going to drive it off a cliff.

That's right. Off a cliff!

In the trailer's script, Carly confronts a monster in the Land of Shadows. The monster, known as the Snidious Nurk, was what one might imagine if a squid and a beetle had a baby. Jet-black, low to the ground, hard shell, numerous gooey tentacles protruding from its sides, you get the picture. They needed the Snidious Nurk to chase Carly at high speeds through a dusty and gray expanse, and then they needed Carly to jump on its back and ride it toward a cliff, before leaping off at the last second, causing the monster to plummet to the bottom and explode into a mess of black goo.

They had the other materials to create the monster—black glossy paint, papier-mâché, large metal bowls, silicone tubes, etc. The scene was meticulously storyboarded. And the locations were secured: the abandoned tennis court and a precipice behind Godfrey and Izzy's house. The plan was to cover one side of the tennis court with green screens (aka dyed green sheets), and then film segments of the sequence that would be interspersed throughout the trailer. First the chase. Then the ride. Finally, the plunge, which would serve as the trailer's grand finale.

"It all comes down to the go-kart," Brewster said as they cleaned up the set before dailies. "The entire trailer depends on that sequence."

"How much is left in the budget?" Rosa asked Izzy.

"About eight hundred and seventy-five dollars," Izzy said, consulting her iPad.

"Can we fund the premiere and get a go-kart for that much?" Brewster asked.

"There's a go-kart for sale on Craigslist for about five hundred dollars," Izzy said. "It's at a farm, not too far from here. That's the best deal I can find."

"Which leaves three hundred and seventy-five dollars for the premiere," Brewster said. "Is that enough?"

"It'll be tight," Rosa said.

"Can we perhaps, maybe, possibly go over budget?" Brewster asked.

"No chance," Rosa said firmly.

It seemed weird to him. If she had five thousand dollars, then why couldn't she have a few hundred more? Her family was dripping with cash. But the one thing Rosa always gave him was one thing he had to give her: respect. Whenever Brewster made a firm decision as a director, she didn't argue. She trusted him to make the best choice. Therefore, he was going to trust her.

"We'll make it work," Brewster said. "But for now, let's get a look at what we did today."

Sunday's dailies were held at Brewster's house. Popcorn was popped. Laughs were plentiful. Even a curious Jade popped their head in to check out what was going on, but Brewster shooed them away.

Jade, like everyone else who wasn't part of this tight-knit production, would have to wait for the premiere.

Chapter 27

Find a Way

The week started with a text. On Monday morning when he woke, Brewster noticed a notification on his phone. It was from his dad.

> Got the invite. Sounds big time. Let me check on some things first. Sorry I haven't been around lately. I'll call you.

Anxiety. That was all that the message gave Brewster, which was certainly not what he wanted. Only a firm yes or no would do. That way he would see exactly what mattered to his dad, without any prompting or convincing one way or another. Brewster couldn't reveal any of his feelings on the matter. Partly because he wasn't entirely sure yet of his feelings. But mostly because, like with any good test, there would be no outside help.

Still, he had to respond. He kept it as simple as possible.

He left it at that.

On the bus to school, he sat by Harriet, and the two went over the special effects work that would need to be completed this week, while Izzy and Godfrey listened in and added their ideas, many of which were helpful.

Carly was in the back with the camera, and before they got to school, Brewster slid into her seat for a moment to ask a question. "You've been keeping Warburton off our backs," he said. "And that's so great. Fantastic. But I do need a few shots of the exterior of the school and the school buses to use in the trailer. Think you could be our second unit director and film stuff like that sometime this week?"

Carly considered it for a moment, then said, "I'll see what I can do."

Good enough. Brewster wouldn't press her on it. The shots weren't essential, even though he wanted them in the trailer. Rosa's advice to *keep our star happy* seemed to be working, so he was going to continue to follow it.

Brewster kept their star even happier by letting Carly skip their recess meetings again. Which wasn't an issue. The pirate ship was only so big, and they didn't need too many opinions contradicting each other. Especially now that they were crunched for time. They had a week until the premiere on the following Monday. There was a lot left to do.

"The farmer with the go-kart will hold it for us until Friday afternoon," Izzy said. "But it's cash only. Will that be a problem?"

"I don't think so," Rosa said. "But it might take a few days."

"Why so long?" Godfrey asked.

"Because it's not like she's got all that money in a piggy bank," Brewster said in Rosa's defense.

She nodded silently.

"As long as we have it by Friday, we're good," Izzy said. "Our parents can help us pick it up with the van."

"And the red carpet?" Brewster asked.

"I'll order it and ship it to your house," Rosa said. "I found one that comes with some velvet rope too."

"As it should," Godfrey said.

That worked for Brewster. And to make sure everyone was on the same page, he summarized the week's responsibilities out loud.

"Rosa will handle the money for the go-kart and the premiere. Harriet and I will keep working on the editing and special effects after school. Godfrey and Izzy will construct the Snidious Nurk. Carly will do whatever Carly does. And Liam . . ."

Eyes and smile wide, hands clasped together, Liam waited for his instructions.

"I've got some green dye, and we need about twenty green sheets so we can turn the fence of the tennis court into a giant green screen," Brewster told him. "Do you think you can find at least twenty sheets and dye them green in the next few days? You know, without spending any money?"

Liam didn't even think about it. "I'll find a way," he said.

"That's the spirit," Brewster replied. "Let's make that our motto, okay?"

They did and it was. They would all "find a way." For the rest of the week, the gang got to work, reporting back on their accomplishments each day at the pirate ship.

In the evenings, Brewster edited footage, then forwarded anything that needed special effects or digital manipulation to Harriet. The Tarkingtons constructed the Snidious Nurk and cleared the forest near the cliff so they could film the monster's death plunge without any obstructions. Liam went door-to-door, asking for sheet donations. He obtained a total of thirty-five ratty and stained sheets that he bleached, then dyed them green in a kiddie pool in his backyard, while his neighbors looked on in puzzlement. His forearms attained the hue of fresh string beans, but he considered it a badge of honor. Grunt work was the life for him.

Brewster's dad sent Brewster a few more texts that week, with messages like:

> I'll call you soon

Or:

> We should set up a time to talk

But since they were neither questions that needed answers nor a definitive yes or no to the invitation, Brewster ignored them. There were so many other things on his mind.

By Friday, Brewster and the rest of the gang had sent out all their invitations to the premiere, which was scheduled for exactly three days later. Monday. Memorial Day. In other words, very soon! Friends, family, classmates, and teachers were included on the list, which had grown to about fifty people. One of Brewster's old elementary school friends even stopped him in the hall to share his enthusiasm.

"That premiere sounds epic," Elijah told him. "Can I bring anything?"

"Just your willingness to be amazed!" Brewster said with excitement. Which was probably overselling things.

But Elijah didn't know that. "Awesome. I'm looking forward to it," he said with a smile, and went on his way.

Brewster was looking forward to it too, but his main concern was Saturday, which would be their last day of shooting. Almost everything was ready. All they needed was that go-kart. The plan was for Rosa to give the Tarkingtons an envelope of cash at the pirate ship at recess on Friday and then after school they'd travel, via their family's van, to the farm where they would buy it and then bring it home. But Brewster was forgetting something important about videos and movies and trailers and life in general.

Things rarely go to plan.

Chapter 28

Best Laid Plans

When the Tarkingtons arrived at the pirate ship on Friday afternoon, they were both on the verge of tears.

"Oh no, what is it?" Harriet asked.

"It's our parents," Godfrey said.

"Did something . . ." Liam gulped. "Happen to them?"

"Worse," Izzy said. "The van broke down this morning. There's no way they can drive us to get the go-kart."

This was not worse than something happening to their parents, but it was indeed troubling. The easiest solution seemed to be for Brewster to ask his mom or Jade for a ride. Unfortunately, they were both busy after school. His mom had a spin class and drinks with friends, and Jade was attending their senior BBQ at the reservoir.

"How late will the farmer hold on to it?" Brewster asked.

"Five p.m.," Izzy said. "There's another interested buyer, and if we don't hand off the cash by then, it's gone gone gone."

"Could we, like, show them the money?" Harriet asked.

"Show! Me! The money!" Liam shouted, but no one reacted because no one knew what he was talking about. He shrugged and explained, "It's from a movie."

It sounded vaguely familiar to Brewster, but he wasn't concerned with movie quotes at the moment. The go-kart was all that mattered. "What do you mean by 'show them the money'?" he asked Harriet.

"I mean we take a picture of the cash, so the farmer knows we have it, and maybe that'll give us some extra time," Harriet said.

"We kinda need the cash first, though," Izzy said. "Which means we need Rosa. Where is she, by the way?"

This question had undoubtedly been on all their minds. Rosa usually spent every minute of recess at the pirate ship. First one there, last one to leave. She was on board whenever they needed her. But now? Nowhere to be seen.

"She wasn't in any classes today," Liam said.

Brewster was embarrassed to admit he hadn't noticed. Any free moment he had during school was spent with his eyes and pen on sheets of paper hidden in his lap, as he examined and revised the shot list for Saturday. The rest of his classmates could've evaporated into thin air, and he wouldn't have been any the wiser.

"So where is she?" Godfrey asked.

It was at that moment that Carly arrived at the pirate ship with an answer. She was panting like she had run all the way there, and when she climbed up on deck, Brewster noticed she wasn't carrying the camera, as had become her custom.

"This . . . isn't . . ." She took a deep breath. "Good."

"Did your parents' van break down too?" Harriet asked.

Carly shot Harriet a strange look, then wiped her brow, took one more breath, and gathered herself. "No, my mom drives a 4Runner," she said. "Very reliable. This is about Rosa. She came to my house last night and took the camera. I didn't think anything of it. But then she stayed home sick from school today. And I just got this text from her."

Carly held up the phone for everyone to see.

> sorry—no more money—no more me—i quit

What in the . . . ?

Brewster seized the phone to get a closer look. He read the message again to make sure he wasn't missing something.

> sorry—no more money—no more me—i quit

It shouldn't be. It couldn't be. It made absolutely no sense.

"She has the camera?" he asked.

"Yep."

"And she *just* sent you this message? Like, right now?"

"Timestamp don't lie."

He read it one more time,

> sorry—no more money—no more me—i quit—

and then Carly snatched her phone back.

It hurt. More than Brewster could possibly imagine. The quitting, obviously. And, of course, the loss of the money. But there was something worse, something far more personal. He was the director. All the responsibility was on his shoulders. So why on earth didn't Rosa tell him first?

"Did you text back?" Brewster asked.

"Did you tell her we need that money?" Izzy asked.

"Did you say we need that go-kart?" Godfrey asked.

"Hold on, hold on," Carly said, tapping her phone. "I'm texting her right now, asking her if this is a joke."

"Rosa isn't good at jokes," Brewster said, still in a daze of emotion and confusion.

"I didn't say it was a good joke," Carly said as her phone chirped with a reply. She held it up again.

> not a joke—i'm done.

Brewster covered his face with a hand. How could this be possible? Rosa was the one who had essentially started this production. If it wasn't for her, Brewster would've already finished the video for "What Do You Do with Friends Who Don't Return Your Messages?" He would've posted it online and watched it either go viral or go nowhere. He would've moved on to the next ten-second video and then on to the next. He would've kept on chasing his million views. And who knows? Maybe he would've caught them by now.

But that didn't happen. Because now he was fully invested in something so much bigger, so much more important. And the main person who led him there? She was bailing on him!

With his hand balled into a tight fist, Brewster pounded the frame of the pirate ship. "We need to go to her house. We need to get that camera. The money! It's three days until the premiere. We need to demand that she un-quit."

"Un-quit?" Carly said, eyebrows up.

"Yes," Brewster said. "Un-quit. Rejoin. Try again. Stop doing whatever it is she's doing."

"Does anyone know where she lives?" Harriet asked.

"Carly does," Brewster said. "They're, like, best friends."

"I wouldn't go that far," Carly said under her breath.

It was loud enough that Brewster could hear her. And once again he had to wonder what was going on between the two girls. "Well then, how far would you go?" he asked.

"To her house," she said firmly. "I'll go to her house. I'll talk some sense into her."

"We need to get the go-kart by five," Izzy said. "Is there enough time?"

"Probably not," Brewster said. "We can't risk waiting for Rosa. Can anyone else drive us? Because my mom and Jade can't."

Heads shook.

"My family has to go to my sister's lacrosse game," Liam said. "It's the playoffs."

"And I have a babysitter," Harriet said. "Mom and Dad are going ax throwing. Which is both romantic and dangerous!"

"Let's not forget the money," Izzy said. "Anyone have five hundred dollars cash right now?"

Heads shook again.

But in Brewster's shaking head, he was considering other options. Because that's what good directors do. He was remembering a promise that someone made to him.

I'm always here if you need me.

He hoped that promise held true.

Chapter 29

Piper at the Gates of Dawn

After standing on the front porch of Piper Barnes's house for a few minutes, Brewster finally built up the courage to knock on the door. A few seconds later, it opened.

"Oh, hi, Mrs. Barnes," Brewster said.

Piper's mom was not what you would typically call an intimidating woman. She was short and thin with hair pulled back into a tight ponytail. She typically wore fashionable workout clothes that always matched, and a smile that Brewster rarely trusted. Why didn't he trust it? Hard to say. Maybe it was because her eyes didn't smile too.

"Good afternoon, Brewster," she said. "What can I do for you?"

"I'm looking for Piper."

"Me too," her mom said with a sigh. "Me too."

Brewster echoed the sigh. "Okay. Can you please tell her I stopped by when she gets home?"

That untrustworthy smile emerged, and Mrs. Barnes said, "Oh, she's here. Up in her room. I just don't know where her head is at these days."

Brewster didn't fully understand what she was talking about, but when she pointed to the stairway and stepped to the side, he knew this was an invitation.

"Thank you," he said, and he entered the house, which smelled like oranges and bleach.

It'd been a few years since he'd been in the Barnes home, but he used to visit quite a bit back in elementary school. Even though Piper was only three years older, she would babysit Brewster from time to time, his parents dropping him off whenever Jade was unavailable to watch him. He and Piper would usually sit together in front of the TV, watching something that was a cartoon, but tolerable for most ages. Pixar. Anime. That sort of thing.

He'd been in Piper's room before, so he knew where it was— up the stairs, down the hall, to the left. But her mom insisted on leading him there anyway. When they reached the door, which was covered in stickers from ski resorts, Piper's mom rapped on it with her knuckles and announced, "You have a little visitor," before flashing that smile one last time, and escaping to the back of the house.

"Brewster?" Piper said when she opened her door. "Did you wander into the wrong house?"

"No," he said. "I need your help."

Piper scanned his eyes like a doctor searching for disease, and then she placed a hand on his shoulder. "Of course."

As soon as he stepped into her room, he started talking. He told her everything. The entire story of the trailer and how it came to be. He told her about Carly and Rosa and the Tarkingtons and Harriet and Liam. He told her about Palivar and the Sprite and, most of all, the Snidious Nurk, because it all came down to that. It was all about the go-kart.

". . . and if we don't get the go-kart by five, it'll be gone and everything will be ruined because the invitations are already sent, and the premiere is in three days and the trailer won't have the best part and—"

Piper put up a hand to stop him. "What do you want me to do?"

"Well," Brewster said. "You said that you were here if I needed you."

"I am."

"Can you ask your mom to drive me, maybe?" Brewster said. "You know, to the farm, to get the go-kart?"

He might as well have been asking her to eat fried worms. Her face twisted up in disgust. "No," she said. "No. No. No."

Brewster hung his head. "Okay. Maybe you didn't mean—"

"I meant what I told you," Piper said. "I'm going to help you. But another way. How far is it to this go-kart farm?"

"Garlic farm, actually," Brewster said. "But they have a go-kart. It's ten miles . . . or probably close to fifteen?"

"Show me the address."

He showed her a Google map with a pin on his phone. She used a thumb and a finger to zoom out and then she whispered to herself. "No mountain passes, no highways. Good."

"What's good?"

"Let me grab some things," she said. "You're coming with me."

● ● ●

A few minutes later, Piper was pedaling her mountain bike away from town, pulling her two-wheeled baby trailer behind it. The weight limit on the trailer was one hundred pounds. Enormous for a baby, but about average for a twelve-year-old boy. With his knees to his chest, Brewster sat inside it like some overgrown toddler being carted off to daycare.

Piper was huffing and puffing, but she was managing. She'd never pulled a twelve-year-old boy "probably close to fifteen miles" but that wasn't because she couldn't do it. She was fit and experienced. She was prepared. This was simply the first time that such an occasion had arisen.

Yes, it was uncomfortable for Brewster, but he couldn't deny that parts of it were fun. The wind in his face. The farms and fields, thick with freshly tilled earth and wildflowers, racing by. He even pulled out his phone to film. Maybe it wasn't right for the trailer, but he could use it for something. It was a lovely afternoon.

"How ya . . . doin' . . . back there?" Piper asked through grunts as she powered them up a hill.

"I'm fine," Brewster said guiltily.

He could imagine how this must've looked: a young woman chauffeuring an able-bodied boy who was probably the same weight as her, in a bike trailer meant for someone who napped with a pacifier. In other words, not good.

Explaining it wouldn't have been much better: "Listen, she's only bringing me a few towns over so I can buy a go-kart, which I plan to turn into a monster and then ride off a cliff. Totally understandable, right?"

Luckily, explanations weren't necessary because they didn't have time to chat with anyone. Sure, they received a few strange looks from drivers who slowed down to get a load of the scene. But before those people could even ask, "Need any help?" Piper would shout, "We're fine, thank you! Move along."

In truth, it would've made a bit more sense to accept a ride from some passing good Samaritan. Brewster was well aware of stranger danger, and wasn't about to start hitchhiking, but some of the drivers were his neighbors. He knew them.

Piper would have none of it, though. She was in her element, chugging along the rural roads, over cracked pavement, pebbles, and dirt. Sweat dripped. Her teeth were clenched so tight that Brewster could practically hear them grinding. The challenge excited her. And when they finally arrived at a weed-eaten gravel driveway that led up to a small garlic farm called the Gates of Dawn, she tipped her head back and started laughing.

Not simply chuckling. Cracking up.

"What's so funny?" Brewster asked as he contorted his body so he could lift himself out of the trailer.

"It's not that it's funny," Piper told him. "It's that I did it. I actually did it!"

"Doesn't surprise me," Brewster said. "You're a really great cyclist."

"I'm adequate," Piper replied, and then she grabbed him by the wrist. "Come on. Let's get your go-kart."

• • •

The farmer was a woman named Marlee Howser, and she didn't look much like a farmer. At least not like the ones in picture books—with straw hats and pitchforks—or in John Deere advertisements—with baseball caps and five o'clock shadow. She was probably in her sixties and wore a stained T-shirt and long basketball shorts, and she sat in a camp chair on her unmowed lawn with her fingers wrapped around a tall can of Twisted Tea.

"Happy weekend," she said, raising the drink in salute as the two kids approached.

"We're here for the go-kart," Piper announced.

"That so?" Marlee said.

"You didn't sell it already, did you?" Brewster asked.

"Is one of you Izzy?"

"No," Brewster said. "But I work with her."

That gave Marlee a good laugh. A laugh that she then extinguished with a long sip of her drink. She pointed over her shoulder with her thumb. "It's by the chicken coop. Tuned up and fueled up. Ready to roll. All I need is the money that your 'coworker' promised."

"About that . . ." Brewster said.

"You don't have the money, do you?" Piper whispered.

Brewster had told her nearly everything, but he had neglected to tell her this. The reason was obvious. He wasn't sure she would've brought him here if she knew he couldn't pay.

"I was hoping we could come to an arrangement," Brewster told Marlee.

"You can't work off the debt pickin' garlic, if that's what you mean," Marlee said. "It's cash on the barrelhead or no deal."

There was no barrel in sight, so Brewster assumed this was some sort of farming expression.

"We'll have the money soon," he told her. "But maybe in the meantime I can help you out. I'm basically a director. I could film a video for you. Like a commercial. To put on your social media accounts. That's worth something."

Another laugh from Marlee. She took another long sip of her drink. "Someone else might need that, but all I got is a Facebook I haven't looked at in ten years. So no thank you. Cash or check will do. You seem like a nice kid, but five hundred dollars is five hundred dollars."

"Brewster, Brewster, Brewster," Piper said, shaking her head.

"I know, I know, I know," he said, hanging his.

"You come all the way out here, and you don't have money?" Piper asked him. "Or even a plan? That's not the Brewster I know."

"Sometimes you just gotta hope things will work out," he said with a sigh. "And sometimes they don't."

It should've seemed inevitable. Showing up without money was only going to lead to one place: disappointment. But Brewster had been lucky in so many ways lately. With his amazing cast and crew, with dodging Warburton, with this entire opportunity Rosa had given him to create something worthwhile. The quest for a million views had made him too cocky, perhaps. Or maybe it was that he had far too much faith in himself. And as that faith drained away, so too did the color from his face.

Marlee obviously noticed, because she clucked her tongue and said, "I wish I could give it to you, kid. I really do. But I've held it for long enough, and I need to sell it. I'm sure another will pop on the market in the next few weeks."

"I don't have a few weeks," Brewster said.

"You entering a race or something?" Marlee asked.

"Trust me, you don't wanna know what his plans are for it," Piper said.

"Not the best getaway car if you're lookin' to rob a bank," Marlee said with a wink. "Seriously, though, whatever you and this Izzy person are up to is gonna have to wait. Apologies that it didn't work out."

Piper patted him on the shoulder. "I guess you can chalk this up as a learning experience."

Brewster had learned plenty over the last couple weeks. More than his brain could handle, frankly. The only thing this moment had taught him was that maybe the universe was working against him. Perhaps the universe was teasing him by letting him get this far and then laughing at him when it was all taken away.

"Let's just go," Brewster said, kicking at gravel and then heading back toward the bike.

That's when Piper grabbed him by the shoulder. "Wait. You might not have come prepared. But I did."

"What does that mean?"

"You're having a premiere, right?"

"We're trying."

"Will there be a poster, with everyone's names and stuff?"

"If Harriet has time to make one."

"Okay," Piper said, and she reached into her pocket. "Here's the deal. Invite me to the premiere. Put my name on the poster. And pay me back, whenever that's possible. Or don't."

"Umm . . . you . . . ?"

She pulled her hand out of her pocket to reveal a blank check with her name at the top. "All I need is a pen."

Chapter 30

Steve McQueen

With a five-hundred-dollar check in hand, Marlee wished them both good luck and went inside to "celebrate with some fajitas."

Brewster, still gobsmacked by Piper's generosity, silently ran his hand over his new go-kart, with its black studded tires, its blue bucket seat, and its red metal frame. Even without getting behind the wheel, he could tell this was a much more powerful machine than the ones he'd ridden at county fairs and amusement parks.

"I don't know if I deserve this," he said.

"Sure you do," Piper told him. "You gave me my bike."

"That bike isn't worth even close to five hundred dollars," Brewster said.

"It is to me," Piper told him. "When I'm riding it, I feel safe. I feel more like myself than when I'm doing anything else.

That's worth . . . so, so much."

As she said it, she looked infinitely pleased, so different than she looked a few nights before, when she sat on her porch with her face lost in sadness. He didn't want there to be another night like that. He wanted Piper to always feel safe.

"If you're happy, then that makes me happy," Brewster told her. "And I don't know what's going on with you at home, but I still worry that I should . . . I'm . . . I don't know . . ."

"We're not getting along at all," Piper said plainly. "Me and my mom. That's what's going on."

"What about your dad?" Brewster asked.

"I'm okay with my dad, but he wants me and my mom to 'fix our issues together.' I don't know how to fix them. I don't know if I even want to fix them. But this?" She waved her arms around, indicating the situation they were in. "This is something I can fix, and this is something I want to fix. So let me. The money is only money I saved. Not for anything special. I have a bike. I have a neighbor who's looking out for me. What else do I need?"

"I don't know. Your own go-kart?"

"Your movie . . . I'm sorry, your trailer . . . it's gonna be amazing, Brewster," she said. "But not because of a go-kart. Because of you."

It was one of the nicest things anyone had ever said to him, and buying the go-kart was one of the nicest things anyone had ever done for him. He didn't know how to respond other than to echo what Piper had said to him when he gave her the bike all those years ago.

"Thank you, thank you, thank you, thank you," he told her, though it didn't feel like nearly enough thank-yous.

Piper smiled, then cocked her chin and asked, "So, are you ready?"

"For what?"

"To drive this thing home."

It was likely illegal. It was definitely unsafe. But the go-kart wouldn't fit in the bike trailer, so what other choice did Brewster have? Actually, he probably had a lot of other choices, but at that moment, this was the only one he would consider. He climbed into the seat and pulled on the helmet he had worn during the ride over.

"Wait a sec," a voice called out. It was Marlee. She was running from the house toward them. When she was within a few yards, she tossed Brewster a pair of old ski goggles and said, "For the bugs."

• • •

About ten minutes later, black flies were splatting against those goggles and the go-kart was kicking up dust and gravel from the road. Brewster was racing home. He had driven slowly at first, right alongside Piper for a couple miles as he got a feel for the machine. That is, until she told him to "Go on ahead. Not too fast. But fast enough to get home before we get into trouble. If you need me, call me."

His phone was attached with bungee cords to the frame of the go-kart, so Brewster could follow the Google Map. Whenever he heard or saw a car approaching, he pulled off to the side of the road—for safety and to make sure no one scolded him or asked him if he had a driver's license. Did he need a driver's license? He wasn't sure, and he didn't want to find out.

When he was more than halfway home, his phone rang. Assuming it was Piper, he quickly pulled over into the dirt parking lot for a trailhead. A closer look revealed the actual caller.

DAD.

This was a call he'd been expecting. And dreading. He debated picking it up and simply asking, "Are you coming or not?" and then hanging up when he got his answer. But he didn't even want an answer at that point. He wanted to keep up the momentum. To finish what he had started.

So he sent the call to voicemail and when his phone chirped, announcing the message's new existence, he decided he couldn't deal with the distraction. He deleted it without listening. Then he safely guided the go-kart back out into the road. He was off again, speeding through the countryside, face flush and heart fluttering.

He didn't go home. Instead, he went directly to the Tarkingtons' house because that was where the go-kart needed to be. When he pulled into their driveway, the entire family ran over from their picnic table, which they had been setting for dinner. They descended upon him, hands clasped in excitement.

"He got it!" Mr. Tarkington exclaimed. "Huzzah!"

"How'd you get it?" Godfrey asked.

"You didn't steal it, did you, Brewster?" Mrs. Tarkington asked.

"But you didn't *not* steal it, did you, Brewster?" Izzy said, her voice full of mischievous delight.

Pulling off the goggles and helmet, wiping the dust from his chin, and hoisting himself up out of the bucket seat, Brewster said, "No, I didn't steal it. We have a new producer who paid for it, but we're not getting any more money, so we gotta get by with what we have."

Mr. Tarkington, with his hair pulled back into a ponytail and half his face covered by large, green-tinted glasses, bobbed his head like he was grooving to some music that only he could hear. "Let me be the first one to say you look positively fierce, Brewster. Wearing the dirt of the road. That piercing stare. An absolute demon behind the wheel."

"You look like Steve McQueen," Mrs. Tarkington added.

The name didn't ring a bell with Brewster, but he could tell it was a compliment, so he said, "Thank you."

"I will concede that he does look a tad better than normal," Godfrey said. "You've done good, my friend."

"Let's keep doing good," Brewster said. "Where's the Snidious Nurk?"

It was in their garage, which served as their workshop. Brewster and the Tarkingtons lugged it out to the yard, and together they attached it to the go-kart. It wasn't long before everything was fitting into place.

At one point, Piper texted Brewster to make sure he got home safe and sound. He assured her that he did, and invited her to the next morning's shoot, but she declined.

> Name on the poster and an invite to the premiere is all I want.

Brewster's mom texted too, asking where he was and what toppings he wanted on his pizza. When he told her that he was at the Tarkingtons' and that he was eating with them, she responded with the heart emoji.

He did eat with the Tarkingtons. Tacos, which was apparently what they ate for almost every meal. Sometimes they ate Mexican tacos, but other times they ate Korean tacos, or spaghetti tacos, or cuisines you would never assume would be tacos but still fit inside a tortilla.

"Every type of food and nutrition you need is in tacos," Izzy explained, and the rest of the Tarkingtons nodded as they munched on their bratwurst and sauerkraut "German tacos."

When the Snidious Nurk was finished, Brewster prepared to return home for the evening. That's when Godfrey asked him something he didn't expect.

"Since you'll be coming here tomorrow morning anyway, would you like to sleep over?"

"Um . . ."

"Apologies if it's too last-minute," Godfrey said. "I've never asked someone to sleep over before, so I don't know the proper etiquette."

"I don't know either," Brewster responded. "Because I've never been asked. But yes. Yes, I'd like to stay. If it's okay with your parents."

"They're the ones who suggested it," Godfrey said. "But I'm glad they did."

Brewster's mom was happy to give her blessing too. And so it was that Brewster found himself attending his very first sleepover, which would've seemed like an impossibility only a week before.

That's not to say it felt normal now. It was weird for Brewster to be on an air mattress in Godfrey and Izzy's room, looking up at the cluttered chaos that was so different from his stark, utilitarian space. But it was inspiring too, because it gave him all sorts of ideas on how to improve his room. It was also comforting to discover that while he and Godfrey were different, they weren't all that different.

Izzy fell asleep early, but the two boys stayed up late, talking about the trailer, and Rosa, and what the heck was going on with her. They sent her numerous messages, none of which she answered. They tried Carly too. No response. And since neither of them knew what else to do, they focused on other things, chatting about TV shows and movies, sharing and debating opinions. Rather than dismissing each other, like they might've done in the past, they truly listened.

"Do you like *Stranger Things*?" Brewster asked, because he liked it a lot, and used it as a point of reference for how the trailer was going to look.

"Not really," Godfrey said.

"Why not?"

"Because all the world-building is borrowed from other things. It's more like a collage than a creation."

"That's sorta why I like it," Brewster said. "It takes all this stuff I love and builds a big story around it."

"Okay, so then you must love that about *Star Wars* too, right?" Godfrey asked. "It's all westerns and samurai swords and sci-fi. *Star Wars* is the best at using old things and making them new."

"I don't like *Star Wars* at all," Brewster said.

Godfrey put a hand on his chest. "Who doesn't love *Star Wars?*"

"Me, I guess," Brewster said. "It's too much . . . family stuff. I mean this is a whole big galaxy they're in and, like, all the important people are related? I don't know. Maybe *The Rise of Skywalker* will change that."

"It's funny 'cause the family stuff is what appeals to me," Godfrey said. "Connections, lineage, destiny. I enjoy thinking about those things."

They went on like this for a while, until they were too sleepy to talk anymore. Brewster didn't know if it was because he had come to respect Godfrey more over the last couple weeks and that's why they were having such a nice conversation, or if it was because Godfrey had come to respect him. Probably a bit of both. The trailer had made that happen, and even though Rosa wasn't with them anymore, the trailer would go on, because the rest of them wanted it to go on.

It was a nice thought to have before fading off to sleep.

Chapter 31

The Chocolate Milk Shot

When Carly arrived on set at the Tarkingtons' house the next morning, she didn't bring the camera, Rosa, or good news.

"Did you talk to her?" Brewster asked. "What's going on?"

"Don't know," Carly said.

"That's a load of horse pucky," Godfrey said.

"Horse pucky?" Carly asked.

Godfrey didn't explain. He simply replied, "Stop covering for her and tell us what's happening."

"I honestly don't know," Carly said. "She won't talk to me. We're not friends like that."

"What kind of friends are you, then?" Izzy asked.

Carly waited a few moments to speak. "Well, my mom and Ken are friends with her parents, Deb and Reese. They go out to eat and ski and kayak together and stuff. So whenever there's a family barbecue or whatever, the two of us hang out."

Any temptation Brewster had to cry, "Aha, just as I suspected, you were never really friends!" was snuffed out by a feeling of disappointment. Because he wanted them to be friends. For both of their sakes.

"I'm sorry you two aren't really very close," he said.

"Calm down," Carly said. "We like each other fine. Besides, it's not like I had any friends when I moved here. She was kind and generous to me. Pretty much the only kid who was. And none of this would be happening without the two of us, you know?"

"How did this all start, anyway?" Harriet asked. "No one ever told me."

"It started when I dug a hole," Brewster told her.

"Actually, no," Carly said. "It started a day before that when you asked me to star in the video. It was movie night that evening at Rosa's house. They have a screening room in their basement. We were supposed to be celebrating Rosa's thirteenth birthday, but the parents picked the movie. Some strange thing from when they were kids about a girl and a baby and a maze and a guy who sings to fuzzy and gross puppets. Rosa and I were like, '*Oookay*, weirdoes,' and we escaped to get some snacks, and that's when I told her about the video I was gonna do with you. Rosa doesn't usually get excited about stuff, but this basically made her go bananas. She told me that she watches your videos all the time and loves them."

Brewster hardly knew what to do with that information. "Wait. She actually said that?"

"Yeah, but it was kind of a secret. She said that we should convince you to make something bigger, like a trailer, and that's when I got the idea for *Carly Lee and the Land of Shadows*. A few days later she told me she had five thousand dollars, and that sealed the deal."

"Five thousand dollars!" Liam exclaimed. "What is she, the queen of England?"

"I'm pretty sure the queen of England has a little more than that," Carly said. "Nope, Rosa is just a kid whose parents have money. Which means she has money."

"Then what happened to that money?" Godfrey asked.

Carly shrugged. "Beats me. Does it matter now?"

"It doesn't," Brewster said. "Because we don't have it, or the camera, anymore."

"We have the go-kart," Izzy said.

"And our phones," Harriet said.

"And all the props and costumes," Godfrey said.

"And one day for filming, one day for the final edit, and one morning to get ready for the premiere," Brewster reminded them.

It was daunting, to say the least. But . . .

"We'll find a way, right?" Liam said.

There it was. Their mantra: *FIND A WAY.* And the way

they found on that last morning of filming was by using their culinary skills, their ingenuity, and everything else in their arsenal. They immediately got to work.

Liam and Harriet handled craft services, raiding their pantries and preparing a stack of PB&Js and filling a cooler with chocolate milk (and a small thermos with kombucha) to get them through the day.

Izzy and Godfrey covered the fences of the tennis courts with the green screens and mixed up a large batch of black goo and innards that would explode from the Snidious Nurk upon its final impact with the ground.

Brewster and Carly rehearsed her action sequence, going through the complex choreography of running and dodging and weaving and jumping.

They all lent their phones to the cause, for use as cameras. The phones didn't have all the bells and whistles of the movie camera, but they gave them the advantage of a multicamera setup, which meant they didn't have to film as many takes. Which was essential for the final sequence, the death plunge of the Snidious Nurk. They could only film that moment once.

Brewster probably should've asked Harriet if she knew how to drive a go-kart, because when it came time to film, he realized that she was the only person small enough to fit inside the shell of the Snidious Nurk.

"You won't have any eyeholes, but you'll wear earbuds and I'll let you know when to turn or slow down or whatever," Brewster told her. "Will that work for you?"

She flashed him a thumbs-up, which was impressive because the Tarkingtons had covered her entire body in a layer of Bubble Wrap and then outfitted her with Liam's sister's hockey gear (gloves, helmet, pads, mouth guard, etc.) to prevent any injuries. Then she climbed into the seat, and they enclosed her in the papier-mâché shell.

For the next few hours, Brewster barked and whispered instructions, and Harriet listened and drove, and the Snidious Nurk zipped and chased, and Carly sprinted and skittered across the abandoned tennis court. Phones mounted on the fence captured wide shots, and a phone attached by a selfie stick to the Radio Flyer wagon captured tracking shots, and phones hidden on Carly and the go-kart captured POV shots.

After a break for lunch, they moved on to the even trickier segment where Carly leapt onto the back of the monster and rode it like a bucking bronco. Her skateboarding skills and balance were put to good use, but to make sure Carly didn't get hurt, they filmed everything at a much slower speed, including her body movements, which they could speed up later in post.

That meant that while the go-kart was only traveling ten miles per hour during filming, it was going to look like it was going at least thirty miles per hour after they changed the playback speed. And Carly, who performed the scene like a slow-motion mime, would look like an absolute dynamo when the editing was finished.

"Thhhiiisss iiisss sssooo sssiiiillllllyyy," Carly droned as she waved her arms in slo-mo.

"Maybe," Brewster said. "But I can't have anyone getting hurt on the last day. Or on any day. It's my responsibility to keep you safe."

Which he did. All the way through the final shot of the entire production, which Hollywood types often refer to as the *martini shot*, because filmmakers drink martinis in celebration once it's all over. Kids don't drink martinis, of course, so they referred to this as the *chocolate milk shot*.

Here's how it went down.

Liam, Izzy, and Carly stood at the top of the cliff, along with the Snidious Nurk, waiting for their signal. Phones were mounted on trees at various heights and distances to document the plunge. Harriet, Godfrey, and Brewster were down below, along with other phones, capturing lower angles.

When it was time to shoot, Izzy walked over to the edge of the cliff, and held up her clapper board one final time.

"Death of the Snidious Nurk scene, the last scene. Take one, the only take. Roll camera."

As she clapped down the arm, Godfrey started all the phones' cameras at the same time, using an app on the iPad. Izzy scooted out of the way, and Brewster hollered, "And . . . action!"

This was the cue for Liam to reach under the shell of the Snidious Nurk and place a brick onto the gas pedal. As soon as he did, the go-kart took off toward the cliff. Fingers crossed, Brewster whispered to himself, "Come on, come on, come on."

And a few seconds later . . .

Yes! It was airborne!

The glorious black beast arced through the sky, tentacles waving. It was beautiful, but also a little sad to know that this would be its final ride. As the Nurk made its downward descent, Carly appeared at the edge of the cliff, where she cupped her hands around her mouth and delivered the final line. "Eat dirt, you Nurk!"

Hidden inside the monster was a balloon, along with a device made by Godfrey and Izzy's mom, who was a mechanical engineer. The balloon was filled with black goo and chunks of black sponge, and the device was made of springs and nails and designed to eject the shell of the Nurk and pop the balloon upon impact. So when . . .

Bam!

The Nurk hit the ground . . .

Thwack!

The shell popped off and . . .

Splat!

The black goo splattered so high and so wide and so far that it formed a black mist in the bright spring air, a cloud hanging suspended for a moment over Brewster, and then evaporating into nothing.

There was a stunned silence for more than a few seconds.

Until Brewster howled in delight.

Then, like a pack of wild beasts, the others howled too.

It was time for some chocolate milk. And kombucha.

Chapter 32

What You Do with Friends Who Don't Return Your Messages

The next twenty-four hours were a blur. The kids would've liked to enjoy some dailies and a wrap party, but they had neither the time nor the money. The celebrations would have to wait until the premiere. Not to worry, though. It was right around the corner.

Liam and the Tarkingtons oversaw preparations for the premiere, collecting all the chairs, decorations, equipment, and food. Carly joined up with Brewster and Harriet, recording ADR for the scenes where the microphones didn't work as well as needed, or where they wanted to alter the dialogue slightly. As a bonus, she brought along the footage of the school Brewster had asked her to film, the establishing shots of the exterior and school buses. She put in her time and acted like a real pro, and Brewster told her that he appreciated it. She even learned a few things about postproduction, and she told him that she appreciated that.

It was all-hands-on-deck from Saturday evening until Sunday evening, and while Brewster obviously needed to share clips and moments from the trailer with Harriet and Carly, he didn't show them the whole thing from front to back. He oversaw the final edit, or "the final cut," as directors called it. Overseeing the final cut meant that the director made the ultimate decisions about which moments would stay in and which ones would end up "on the cutting room floor" or, in the case of digital editing, at the bottom of the computer's trash can.

Brewster finished his final cut earlier than expected, at around 6:30 on Sunday evening. It was a bit anticlimactic. He could've done more work on it, but he was starting to fear that he was losing perspective, that he was overthinking things. So he saved a copy and stepped away from the laptop like it would explode if he touched it again.

"I . . . I . . . I think that's it," he whispered to himself, hardly believing it.

At approximately the same time, he heard a knock on his front door. He welcomed the distraction and raced downstairs. When he opened the door, he found Godfrey on his porch. Behind the boy, alongside the road, was the Tarkingtons' van, rumbling and alive. Godfrey's parents and Izzy were waving through open windows.

"The van is fixed!" Brewster exclaimed, perhaps as happy about this turn of events as they were.

"We have a mechanic friend who worked on it all weekend," Godfrey said. "That's not the only thing, though."

"What do you mean?"

"He fixed something else, too. Returned it to its former glory." Godfrey stepped to the side, revealing the go-kart on Brewster's lawn. The frame was a little bent and scratched, but it was sparkling clean. Any evidence that it was once a gooey black monster was now long gone.

Godfrey handed the go-kart's key to Brewster. And Mrs. Tarkington called out from the van. "Looking good, Steve McQueen."

Brewster had googled a picture of Steve McQueen earlier. It was nice of her to say, because Mr. McQueen was a handsome man, but Brewster knew he looked absolutely nothing like him.

"We're off to prepare our attire for the premiere," Godfrey said as he hustled back to the van. "It's all coming together, old boy. Can't wait for tomorrow. Can't wait to experience the thrills. Can't wait for everyone to experience the thrills!"

Brewster agreed wholeheartedly. But as the van pulled away, he knew that it wasn't *all* coming together. And he knew that not quite *everyone* was going to experience the thrills. There was at least one missing piece. One missing person. He texted Carly to ask for an address as he rushed inside to grab the ski goggles.

• • •

Twenty minutes later, ski goggles pressed to his face, Brewster was racing the go-kart into the hills. Miles from home, deep in the woods, heading down a private dirt road, he was almost there.

Rosa's house wasn't the monstrosity he expected. It was big, no question, far bigger than his house, but it wasn't gaudy or frightening. It had numerous gables and a wraparound porch. A three-car garage and a flower garden that was beginning to pop to life. It was painted light blue, with a gray roof and white trim. The edge of a pond called out from a distance in the backyard. So too did the edge of a pool. It felt warm, like an inn, or a restored mansion at a living history museum. Ready for guests, in other words. Still, he wasn't sure how happy the Blake family would be to see a dust-covered kid popping in for a hello. So he parked the go-kart behind some bushes near the road and tapped out a message on his phone.

It was the fourth message he'd sent Rosa in the last twenty minutes. These were the first three:

it's done! wanna see it?

if you don't answer i might have to come to your house

i'm coming to your house

His fourth message, which also included a photo of Rosa's house taken from the road, simply said:

i'm here

This one did the trick.

don't move—i'll be right down

Moments later, Rosa was standing, hands on hips, at the edge of her driveway, and Brewster was stepping out from behind the bushes. She didn't say anything until she spied the go-kart.

"You got it?"

"Yep."

"But you didn't crash it?"

"Oh, we crashed it. Busted it up big-time. Wanna see?" He held up his phone.

"Is the trailer really done?"

"I mean, I should probably keep tinkering with it, but—"

"I'm sure it's perfect."

"Have a look." He wagged his phone at her.

She waved it off. "I dropped out. Let other people see it first. I'll see it when you put it on YouTube."

Brewster lowered the phone and gave her a little nod. "Okay. But don't worry. I understand."

"Understand what?"

"Why you quit."

Her eyebrows went up in surprise. "Why'd I quit?"

"You must've spent all the money and felt bad because you didn't give Izzy the right numbers for the budget and—"

"Come on, Brewster. You know better than that. The budget was perfect, but . . ."

"But?"

She sighed and said, "I never had any money."

Was she messing with him? Gaslighting him? She seemed serious, but how could she be? "Of course you had money," Brewster said. "You bought all that stuff."

Rosa sighed again and said, "This is so embarrassing." Then she reached into a sleeve in the back of her phone and pulled out a credit card. When she held it up, Brewster could clearly read her name on it.

"Wait. How'd you get a credit card?"

"If you're thirteen, your parents can get you one. So my parents got me one. For my birthday. To teach me financial responsibility. To order clothes for school. Books. Educational things. And for emergencies."

This must've been something that rich people did, because Brewster had never once assumed that he'd be getting a credit card, at least not until he was in college. Or older.

"It has a five-thousand-dollar limit," Rosa went on. "And the bill posts on the last Tuesday of the month."

"So in two days?"

"Yep. That's why we needed to be done by then. But . . ."

"But?"

"When I tried to use the card to take out cash for the go-kart, I might've done something wrong. The card locked up. The company thought it was fraud."

It wasn't far from that, as far as Brewster was concerned. Cash for go-karts wasn't exactly an educational or emergency expense, even if it did feel like it at the time.

"What'd you tell your parents?" he asked.

"That's the thing," Rosa whispered with a cringe. "Nothing. I don't know if they know yet."

"They'll find out eventually, right?"

She hung her head and nodded slowly. "Like I said, so embarrassing."

Embarrassing and inevitable. Credit cards may seem like free money when you use them. But even kids like Brewster knew that you eventually had to pay them off.

"What were you gonna do when they saw the bill? I mean, what *are* you gonna do?"

Rosa hid her face in her hands. "Deal with the consequences, I guess. I was gonna try to return as much stuff as possible, but I don't have any of the original packaging. It's all clearly used. The camera has chocolate milk fingerprints all over it."

"Sorry," Brewster said, hanging his head a little.

"I thought of buying cryptocurrency and hoping it would go up so I could pay it off."

"That's a terrible idea."

Rosa paced in circles, twirling her fingers through her hair, and saying, "I know, I know. That's why I didn't do it. I didn't do anything. All I cared about was the trailer, so that's all I thought about. Until I was forced to think about this. I couldn't face any of you. It was too difficult."

"I can definitely relate," Brewster said, which was true in so many ways he was aware of, and perhaps in a few ways that he wasn't quite aware of yet.

Rosa finally stopped pacing, and she stared at Brewster, but not how she usually did. She wasn't hiding herself behind steely eyes. She was revealing herself behind soft ones.

"My parents make their money from real estate investments," she said. "It's not evil, but it's not what I consider important. This trailer felt like an opportunity to make something important. Something worthwhile. A real piece of art. With people like you. Friends who are so much more talented than I'll ever be. And that credit card gave me the opportunity. How could I pass it up?"

Brewster knew this was incredibly irresponsible on her part.

Yet her irresponsibility had brought them so far. He'd never seen Rosa this honest, this guilty, and this vulnerable. He wanted to scold her and thank her at the same time.

Instead, he simply told her, "I should've pushed you into a bottomless pit."

"What?"

"For the last few days, you haven't been returning my messages. And that's what you're supposed to do to friends who don't return your messages. Remember?"

This made her smile. "Right."

"You should've told me earlier," he said. "Maybe we could've figured out a solution. And you really need to talk to your parents. Now. As in today. We're having the premiere tomorrow. They should at least know what they're paying for."

"Right," she said again, but this time the word felt so much sadder.

"Do you think you'll be in big trouble?"

"Um . . . yeah. My parents aren't mean. They love me, and they understand when I make mistakes. But they're parents."

The way she said it made it sound like it was universal, like all parents would act the same in this situation. Brewster wasn't so sure about that. But he was sure about one thing. "Trust me," he said. "Talking is always better than avoiding."

"Maybe, but I'm also tempted to hop in that go-kart and make a getaway," Rosa said, and then she crouched down to get a better look at it. "Speaking of which, this thing doesn't have any headlights."

"So?"

Rosa's face registered the concern of someone much older than Brewster. Which made sense. She was thirteen, after all. While he was merely twelve.

"So . . ." she said. "The sun will go down soon, and directors are responsible for the safety of their cast and crew. That includes themselves."

"Which means?"

Her arm shot up, and she pointed to the road. "Which means, get moving."

"Now?"

"Go!"

Chapter 33

A Million Views

As Brewster drove the go-kart away from Rosa's house, another of his dad's voicemail messages popped onto his phone. The irony was not lost on him. He had been avoiding his dad as much as Rosa had been avoiding her parents. If anyone deserved to be pushed into a bottomless pit, it was Brewster. So rather than ignore or delete the message, he would follow his own advice. He would call his father as soon as he got home. One final item to check off the list before the premiere.

But when he pulled the go-kart into his driveway, Brewster noticed a package by the door, and that stole his attention for a moment. It was large and heavy, so he had to drag it across the yard to a shady spot near the barn, where he planned to open it. He had a pretty good idea what it was.

Using scissors to slice through the tape, the cardboard,

and the plastic, Brewster unboxed some velvet rope and, most importantly, the red carpet, which unfurled in front of him like a hound's tongue on a hot day. He felt guilty about it at first, knowing that he should probably return it so that the money would go back on Rosa's credit card. But from the moment the bottom of the carpet hit the dirt, he knew he was keeping it.

As he repositioned it in the yard to see how it would look leading from the driveway to the barn, Jade stepped out from the back door of the house and walked over to join him.

"It's pretty," Jade said.

"It's exactly like I imagined it would be," Brewster responded, still staring at it.

"I'm glad," Jade said, and then motioned with their chin toward the crew chairs that were set up in the barn. "Come talk to me for a sec."

"Okay," Brewster said, and he followed Jade inside. Brewster chose his director's chair, obviously, and Jade sat in Liam's chair, which was amusing for some reason. That's why Brewster was smiling when Jade broke what sounded like bad news.

"I'm sorry. But he's not coming."

Brewster held on to the smile for as long as he could as he asked a question he already knew the answer to. "You mean Dad?"

Jade nodded. "He wanted to tell you himself, but you haven't been responding to his messages."

Brewster gulped and nodded. Guilty as charged.

"Again, I'm sorry, Brew," Jade went on. "I know this premiere is really important to you. But Mom will be there. So will I."

It *was* important to him, and he was glad that his mom and Jade would be there. That was expected, though, because they were home. And it didn't answer a question that was weighing on Brewster's mind.

"When did you figure out that our family is different?" he asked Jade.

"How do you mean?"

"I mean, all families are different. I know that. But ours is *really* different. Like, Dad is out there in Portland spending time with some other lady, isn't he?"

This made Jade laugh, but not a happy laugh. A resigned laugh. "I don't know about that. Maybe he is, but—"

"And if it's an affair or something, I don't think I care," Brewster said firmly. "Really. It doesn't matter to me. But what worries me is that I *should* care. Right?"

"I don't know about that either."

"Dad accidentally sent me a message with a picture of him and her. It wasn't meant for me. I wondered for a while about who the message was actually meant for, until I finally figured it out."

"Who?"

"I'm pretty sure it was meant for Mom. Because Mom

doesn't care either. Neither do you. So it's not only Dad who's the problem. It's all of us."

Jade sat with the idea for a moment, staring out of the barn at who knows what, until they finally turned to Brewster and stated, "This is who we are. We're used to this. It's always been like this."

"Has it? Because I remember doing stuff together. Swimming. Picnics. New York City. Not all the time. But sometimes."

"When you were little, Mom and Dad tried for a bit to do the traditional family thing. Didn't work for them. They can't change. This is them."

And this was Brewster. Still confused. Still needing answers. "So why the heck do they stay married?"

"I don't know. Us?"

"Us?"

Jade laughed again, but this time the laugh had a little more light to it. "Okay, maybe it's for insurance. Or maybe they still enjoy each other's company. Only not all the time, or in the way that other parents do. Honestly, I don't fully understand it."

"But you're supposed to understand it."

"Why? Because I'm seventeen?"

"Sure."

"That's not very old."

"Older than twelve."

"Doesn't feel like it sometimes."

"Really?"

Jade nodded and sniffled and said, "I want to make sure you're okay, Brew. That your premiere wasn't all an excuse to make sure Dad came home."

Brewster had certainly wondered this himself, and he had eventually come to a conclusion. "No," he said. "It was an excuse to make sure he wouldn't come home."

This deflated Jade. First their shoulders sagged, then their face. This made them so sad. "Oh, Brew," Jade said.

"What? I'm fine."

"You can be upset by this. It's perfectly normal to be upset."

"Maybe I'm not perfectly normal," Brewster said with a shrug.

And as far as he was concerned, the conversation was over. So he stood. As soon as he did, Jade stood too. Then Jade hugged their little brother. Very tightly.

Neither of them said *I love you*, or anything for that matter, but that's what the hug felt like. Like love. It lasted only a few seconds, and then Jade let Brewster go.

"I'll be okay," Brewster assured them.

"I know," Jade replied. "But remember, you don't have to be like Mom and Dad. You can have any sort of life or family. You can be whoever you need to be."

Need was the important word here. Not whoever you *want* to be. Need.

"Thank you," Brewster said, genuinely.

Then the two split off. Jade went to do whatever it was that Jade did on Sunday evenings, while Brewster rolled up the red carpet, stored it safely in the barn, and then hurried to his room.

Though he was tempted to sit at the MacBook and tinker with the trailer some more, he chose to crawl under his covers instead. He had his phone with him, with the voicemail from his dad at the top of his notifications. Staring at the ceiling, blanket to his chin, he finally listened to it.

"Hey, buddy. Not sure if you've been getting my messages, but I think you can probably guess that I'm not gonna make it to that movie thing tomorrow. Too much work. Too far to come. You understand, I'm sure. I'll be home soon, though. To give your mom a break for a bit, you know? She could use some time away too. Maybe you and I can watch some movies together when I get back. Anyway, sorry I can't be there. I'll keep an eye out for it online. Good luck!"

It would've been a fine message if it were sent by a friend. A cause for disappointment, maybe, but understandable. This wasn't from a friend, though. This was from a father.

Brewster tried to imagine Godfrey and Izzy's father sending such a message, or Harriet's father bailing on her big event. He didn't know Rosa's or Liam's fathers, and all he knew about Carly's father was that he didn't treat her well. But he was confident that these dads would've handled the situation differently.

How, exactly? Brewster wasn't sure. There were a million

ways to look at it. A million views. And Brewster had just the one. His dad, his family, his life. His view.

It was getting dark in his room. The golden hour had passed. As he lay in bed, a knotty feeling moved from Brewster's chest to his throat to his face. He had absolutely no control over what came next.

He began to cry. To weep, actually. Big tears, and whimpers, and gasps. A flood of the strongest emotion possible overtook him. It felt terrible and wonderful all at once. It felt essential, like water or air. It felt like darkness and light. And when it was over, Brewster rolled onto his side and fell into a deep sleep.

Chapter 34

Winner Winner Chicken Sandwich

Brewster dreamt that night, and he remembered his dream again. It was a simple dream. Like his Winner Winner Chicken Dinner dream from a couple weeks before, it started with Brewster in bed, laptop in front of him, reviewing his YouTube videos. Only this time he was looking at the trailer for *Carly Lee and the Land of Shadows*. It's not surprising that his eyes immediately moved to the number of views at the lower left-hand corner. And wouldn't you know it . . .

1,111

Exactly like in the other dream. And like in the other dream, the numbers started to climb, faster and faster, scored to the infectious sounds of slot machines.

5,000 . . . 10,000 . . . 50,000 . . . 100,000 . . . 250,000 . . . 500,000 . . .

Only this time, he didn't look away. This time he watched it race all the way up to . . .

1,000,000.

There. Undisputable. Two commas. Seven figures. A million. A MILLION!

It felt . . .

He wasn't sure how it felt. Because when Brewster did finally look up from the laptop's screen, he noticed that his room was empty. His family wasn't there. There was no one at the foot of his bed chanting, "Winner winner chicken dinner!" There was only, well, a chicken dinner.

Or to be more accurate, a chicken sandwich from Subway, still in its wrapper and sitting on top of his comforter. He didn't even like Subway's chicken sandwiches. Still, he reached to grab it, and when his fingers touched it, the veil lifted. The dream ended. Brewster woke up.

Relief poured over him like it did whenever he woke from a nightmare. He was so much happier to be in the real world. Especially now. Because when he looked up from his bed, he could see out his window, and there, in the yard, starting to set up for the big premiere, were his friends.

● ● ●

Brewster, Liam, and the Tarkingtons worked all morning and past lunch. They hung the Tarkingtons' movie screen inside the barn and positioned the projector for optimum size and resolution. They lined up camp chairs and folding chairs and dining room chairs until they had enough seating for at least fifty people. They strung white Christmas lights around the beams, and they unfolded card tables and covered them with the green screen sheets, so they were ready for refreshments. The refreshments came from everyone's fridge and pantry. No money needed, simply a little bit of this and a little bit of that, cooked up and mixed up and presented in taco form.

Carly couldn't join them because she said she was, in her words, "getting something ready for the big show." And Harriet only popped by when they were nearly finished. She was there to deliver the poster she had been working on all night and all morning. She placed it on an easel near the entrance to the barn and draped a shawl over it until everyone had gathered around.

"Voila!" she said, pulling the fabric away.

The poster was delightful. The medium was charcoal, so black and grays dominated, but it felt more vibrant than depressing. The title, *Carly Lee and the Land of Shadows*, arced across the top, over the head of our heroine, who was depicted in full-on ninja pose. On one side of Carly, set farther back and emerging from smoke, was Palivar the Pitiless, with his cloak and scepter. He looked particularly villainous, a testament to Godfrey's dedicated portrayal and Harriet's ability to capture it. On the other side of Carly, bursting out of a hole, were the creatures from the Land of Shadows: the Sprite, the Snidious Nurk, the Shadowzoids, and so on. At the bottom were the credits, which listed Piper as one of the producers, as promised.

"It's amazing," Izzy said.

"No, it's even better," Brewster said. "It's stupendous. Thank you, Harriet."

"Who gets to keep it when this is all over?" Godfrey asked.

"That's the fun thing," Harriet said. "I'm gonna make one for each of you."

It was touching, unnecessary, and totally Harriet. There would be no talking her out of it. She always kept her promises.

"Thank you," they all said at the same time.

And she replied, "But don't sell yours on eBay, okay?"

Shortly after that, they finished the final preparations. Mason jars with freshly picked flowers scattered around the property, a sign reading "Exclusive Screening!" hanging from the mailbox, and, of course, the velvet ropes and red carpet leading from the driveway to the barn.

Everything was ready, so they all rushed home. To shower. To get dressed. To prepare for the first, but hopefully not last, premiere of their lives. Brewster didn't have far to go, obviously, but he returned to his room and put on his best button-down shirt, some ironed slacks, a black belt, and a shiny pair of black shoes that he had only worn once, to a cousin's wedding. Since he didn't need to travel, and since his mom and Jade had both left the house while the kids were setting things up, Brewster was the first person in attendance.

He was too nervous to sit, so he wandered around the yard. It had been a mere nineteen days since he had finished digging the hole. Less than three weeks. It was unfathomable how much had changed. The hole, however, remained.

He kicked a clod of dirt into it, which quickly landed with a damp thud. It had been so hard to dig and yet it was still so shallow.

Was it all worth it? he wondered. The answer came in the form of enthusiastic voices.

"Wow!"

"Incredible!"

"It's like a dream, isn't it?"

And Brewster turned around to see a group of well-dressed people at the edge of his driveway, starting to walk down the red carpet.

Chapter 35

Live from the Red Carpet!

It was no surprise that it was Liam and his family who arrived first. His mom, dad, and older sister were all dressed nicely, but casually—skirts, dark jeans, polo shirts, sandals, loafers, etc. Liam, on the other hand, was wearing a tuxedo.

"Looking good, buddy," Brewster said as he approached them.

"I found it at a garage sale," Liam told him. "I'm guessing it used to be for a chimpanzee. There was fur on it."

Brewster couldn't help but laugh at this. And Liam's parents couldn't help but offer their thanks.

"Liam is so happy to be involved," his dad said.

"He's always raving about your videos," his mom said.

"I heard there would be tacos," his sister said.

Brewster shook their hands and told them, "We couldn't

have done this without him," which delighted them all, except for Liam's sister, who was more delighted by spotting the spread of tacos in the barn. She rushed over to it.

"It was an honor," Liam said as he shook Brewster's hand. "And I'm sorry if I've been annoying."

Nothing had really changed about Liam. There were still things he did that Brewster found annoying—holding on to a handshake for too long, for example—but who didn't do annoying things? Brewster certainly did annoying things.

Forget all that. Liam was helpful. He was true. He cared. He was a friend.

"You're welcome to come over anytime," Brewster said, which was about the best thing he could've told the boy.

Beaming, Liam finally let go of the handshake and replied, "The chimp who used to wear this tuxedo probably never had it so good."

Then he rushed away, joining his family by the tacos.

Harriet and her family arrived next, and they all greeted Brewster with hugs. Her little sister, Kaia, asked, "When am I gonna be able to help with one of your movies?"

"When your parents say you're allowed to," Brewster responded.

Her father mussed Kaia's hair and said, "When she learns how to tie her shoes."

"And make her bed," her mother told them.

"And render 3D graphics," Harriet added.

Kaia tilted her head and squinted her eyes, then announced, "I can do all that."

If she was anything like her sister, she probably could. Of all the kids who had worked on the trailer, Harriet was the most talented. At least, that's what Brewster thought. But he also knew it would embarrass her to tell her that. So he simply asked, "Do you mind teaching me someday?"

"How to tie your shoes?" Harriet replied.

He wasn't sure if she was serious, but then he looked down. His shoelaces were indeed untied. As Brewster bent to tie them, Kaia began to sing, "Bunny ears, bunny ears, playing by the tree . . ."

A few minutes later, the Tarkingtons arrived in full regalia. Godfrey was dressed as Palivar, and Izzy as the Sprite. Their parents, not ones to be upstaged, were dressed as King Arthur and Guinevere from the old stories about Camelot and the Knights of the Round Table. They looked both ridiculous and amazing, and they immediately began mingling with Harriet and her family, who seemed enchanted by the costumes, asking to feel the fabrics and wield the accessories.

Harriet's poster didn't show all the trailer's credits, but if it had, then the Tarkingtons would've been listed far more than any of the other kids. Izzy had filled about a dozen roles on the crew alone. Her future was undoubtedly bright, no matter what she chose to do in her life, or even tomorrow. Brewster didn't want to bother her at the moment, but he did want to acknowledge her. That's why he had asked Harriet to list Izzy as a producer on the poster. And if they ever worked together again, he vowed to let her "unionize," even though he wasn't entirely sure what that meant.

Piper showed up next, and Brewster noticed that she grinned when she spied her name on the poster too. That moment alone was worth having the premiere. Brewster's mom and Jade weren't far behind Piper, and they started chatting up their neighbor. It looked like a happy conversation, and it looked like a conversation about Brewster, because they kept on peering over at him. It was enough to make him blush. And turn away.

Before long, other guests started to fill the yard and barn. Kids from school were there, including old friends like Tyler, Henry, Elijah, and Luke. Even a few teachers showed up. The art teacher, Ms. Marston. The sixth-grade English teacher, Mr. Hoyt. And, most surprisingly of all, Mr. Warburton. *The* Mr. Warburton!

Who the heck invited him?

He wore the same thing he wore to school every day: brown shoes, khaki pants, and a white collared shirt with a green sweater over it. But he seemed far from comfortable outside his classroom. Lingering by the tacos, he sipped lemonade and kept his head down, until he noticed Brewster. As soon as he did, he motioned for the boy to join him, and having no other choice, Brewster went.

"I'm so glad I received an invitation to this prestigious event," Mr. Warburton told him. "Am I to understand that we'll be watching a trailer for a movie today?"

"Yessir," Brewster said, looking at his feet.

"And do you remember what I said to you? About your drive to succeed?"

Brewster didn't remember the exact words, but it had something to do with being his true self and focusing on the important things in life. That afternoon, Brewster felt as true to himself as he'd ever been. And he could finally look up and be completely honest with his teacher.

"Working on this trailer, with the help of all my friends, helped me understand what's important to me," he said.

And Mr. Warburton smiled and nodded. "Good. Very good. And I look forward to watching it."

There was no mention of the camera. Or the documentary. Or the extra-credit assignment. Mr. Warburton, who had seemed so intimidating for so long, simply stood there smiling and nodding, like a friendly teacher who was simply happy to see a student thriving.

It was at that moment that Carly made her entrance. She was positively radiant in the glittery silver dress she had borrowed from the Tarkingtons. It stood in stark contrast to the attire of the people who accompanied her. There was her mom, Emi, who looked like an older version of Carly, but sporting a green tennis dress, bright white sneakers, and a pink visor. And there was her stepdad, Ken, rocking the board shorts and flip-flops (but also a T-shirt, so perhaps for him this was considered formal attire).

Carly abandoned her family as soon as she spotted Mr. Warburton, and she hurried toward him. He met her halfway and gave her one of those two-handed handshakes that a person reserves for old friends. Brewster was tempted to eavesdrop and see if they were having a similar conversation about the important things in life, but he was distracted by the next person who appeared at the top of the red carpet.

Rosa.

Rosa wore a simple black cotton dress and black shoes and black headband to hold the hair out of her face. Rosa's parents, who arrived with her, wore the crisp and airy clothes that adults wore to nice restaurants and parties, which was another way of saying they appeared more or less normal. Or at least they didn't look like Brewster imagined they might look. They weren't covered in jewelry and silky fabrics like reality-show rich people. In fact, they didn't look all that different from Harriet's or Liam's parents.

When Rosa's mom and dad spotted Carly's mom and Ken, they joined them at the entrance to the barn, exchanging hugs and compliments. Which left Rosa alone to pace slowly down the red carpet with her arms straight at her sides. Brewster hurried over to get the scoop.

"You talked to them?" he asked.

"I did."

"And . . . ?"

"They took my phone for a month. And I have to pay them back. With interest."

"That means more, right?"

"Yeah, but they weren't cruel. It's a fixed rate."

Brewster didn't know what a "fixed rate" meant, but he trusted that Rosa did, and that it was a good thing.

"Were they angry?" Brewster asked.

"Big-time," Rosa said. "I mean, not as much as I thought they'd be. They were mostly mad that I didn't ask. They said they were glad I spent the money on 'something constructive,' though. And they were curious about what we made. That's why they came."

"Think they'll be interested in maybe . . . investing some more money?" Brewster asked in a high-pitched voice indicating that he knew he probably shouldn't be asking.

"Don't push it, Brewster," Rosa said.

So he didn't. Instead, he posed a different question. "Did you come today for the same reason as your parents? Are you curious?"

Rosa gave him that steely stare for a moment, but she couldn't maintain it like she might've in the past. A smile cracked across her face, and she said, "Yeah. I'm a little bit curious."

Brewster smiled back. "Consider yourself lucky, then, because we're about to start."

Chapter 36

The New Kids

Godfrey and Izzy were already in their places, attending to the projector and house lights. But before Brewster could lead everyone into the barn and announce that the show was about to begin, Carly had climbed up on a chair and was using her cupped hands as a megaphone.

"Grab a seat, any seat!" she hollered. Figuring he should join her, Brewster approached, but she stopped him dead in his tracks with a pointing finger and a command. "That includes you, young man. Sit! I have a surprise to share."

A surprise? There had been no discussion of surprises. The premiere had been carefully planned. The trailer was supposed to debut in five minutes. Izzy had written out a schedule and everything.

Brewster was about to shout his objections when he

remembered what Rosa always told him: "Keep our star happy."
Plus, he remembered something about surprises. They weren't
always bad things.

He did as he was told. He took a seat next to his mom and
waited, even though waiting was absolute torture. Meanwhile,
Rosa sat on the other side of him, with her parents nearby. She
leaned over and whispered, "I think I know what's happening."

When the rest of the seats were filled, Carly hopped down
from the chair and moved in front of the screen, from where she
made her next announcement.

"Greetings, ladies and gentlemen. Thank you for coming.
We have a special treat for you today. It's the world premiere of
the trailer for a movie that doesn't even exist: *Carly Lee and the
Land of Shadows!*"

There was clapping. A few cheers and whistles. A nice
response.

"But before we get into that, I'm gonna flip the script on ya,"
she continued. "Usually, you show a trailer before a movie. But
today, we're gonna show you a movie before a trailer!"

This had definitely not been discussed. An entire movie
before the trailer! That would ruin everything. Brewster had to
put the brakes on, so he stood and started to say, "Now, wait a
sec—"

But Carly cut him off. "Don't worry, B-Dog," she said. "This
movie is, like, two minutes long. Won't take any time at all. It's

an appetizer to the main course. So have a seat and enjoy, okay?"

Rosa tugged on Brewster's sleeve, pulling him back down. "Aren't you curious?" she whispered. "Even a little bit?"

He was. Also nervous. And excited. And . . . sweaty. He was a lot of things. And when Carly signaled for Izzy to lower the lights and for Godfrey to turn on the projector, Brewster was in the one place in the world he wanted to be: a dark room, with a crowd, watching light flickering on a big screen.

"Let the show begin," Carly said.

After another round of applause, an image appeared, the first shot of a movie. It was in black and white, and it showed their school from the outside.

Images of school on a holiday weren't what most kids wanted to see, but the ones in the crowd resisted the urge to boo. Which was a good thing because it would've drowned out Carly's voice. As the shot changed to one in the halls, documenting the daily hustle and bustle, she provided narration.

"Hi. My name is Carly Lee. And this is my school. It's not my first school. But it's my school right now. I moved here from New Jersey. I'm a new kid."

A title appeared on-screen in big black letters:

THE NEW KIDS

"This is a documentary about new kids," Carly's voice went on, and the shot shifted to one of the playground and the chaos of recess. *"What do new kids think? What do they feel? What are*

they like? This documentary will tell you. Documentaries are usually boring, but new kids aren't boring, so this documentary won't be boring. Even though it's in black and white!"

It suddenly became clear to Brewster what Carly had been up to over the last couple weeks. She had been filming this documentary. Maybe it had started as a trick to keep Mr. Warburton off their backs, but clearly it had evolved into something else. Something, perhaps, more personal?

The rest of the movie featured quick clips of interviews with "new kids" in their school, from fifth-graders to eighth-graders. They all had things to say, such as:

"I moved here from Virginia."

"I'm from Maine."

"We used to live in Burlington, which isn't far away, but feels far away."

"It's hard making friends."

"I like the lunch here, which is better than my last school."

"I hope we stay awhile."

"Sometimes I cry."

"There's one kid who's made things so much easier."

"It's really hard. There are bullies."

"Maybe my parents will get back together, and I'll move back home."

"I never saw the snow before I got here."

"The teachers are nice."

"I'm learning to ice-skate."

"It's too cold."

"I'm planting a garden."

"I love it here."

"I hate it here."

"It's okay here so far . . . but we'll see."

Brewster didn't know most of the kids in the documentary, but he recognized them. And while Carly wasn't one of the kids being interviewed, she must've related to some of the things they were saying. In fact, she probably related to most of the things they were saying. Her ending narration indicated as much.

"You never know what a new kid is going through, unless you've been a new kid yourself," she said. "And even then, you forget. You don't remember that it's like stepping through a portal and ending up in a whole new dimension. You don't remember your mixed feelings, how at one moment you may want lots of attention, and the next moment you wanna fade into the crowd. It's never easy, even for the ones who make it look easy. So next time you see a new kid, make sure you remember that they're new. And they're going through a lot. Please be nice."

The final shot was of Carly herself, waving at the camera and then hopping on her skateboard, doing a little kick-flip, and riding off into the sunset. This was the only shot in the movie that was in color.

There were no credits other than: *You're amazing, everyone!*

Then the screen went black. The lights went up. Applause.

Brewster was stunned for a moment. It wasn't only that Carly had done a great job; it was also that her documentary had moved him. He had never been "new," and while he didn't relate to everything these kids said, he related to the feeling. Simply visiting his new friends' homes, and meeting their families, had made him feel like a foreigner. Maybe they sensed that. Maybe they didn't. But their welcoming words and actions had done so much to help him realize that there were all sorts of futures available to him. And Carly's documentary made him feel less alone. That certainly deserved applause. So Brewster clapped as loud as anyone.

Carly did a series of bows and curtsies and told the crowd, "I don't want to take up any more time, but I do want to thank my friends for being so patient with me while I worked on this secret documentary. I also want to thank my classmates who shared their stories. And finally, I want to thank Mr. Warburton, who helped me realize that I love interviewing people. And that documentaries don't have to be boring!"

Mr. Warburton rubbed the bridge of his nose with a thumb and forefinger, like he was trying to dam up impending tears. Bubbling with pride and excitement, Carly bounded over and found a seat next to her mom and Ken, who each gave her a high five.

Since Carly didn't say anything else to the crowd, Rosa

leaned over and whispered to Brewster. "I think that means it's your turn."

He thought it meant that too, and it terrified him. Nevertheless, he took a deep breath, and a deep gulp, then stood up and approached the screen. Dozens of expectant eyes followed him. He had no speech prepared. Even if he had written one, he probably wouldn't have been able to deliver it. The audience was smiling, not only because they enjoyed Carly's documentary, but because they wanted to be there. Brewster, however, was trembling. He could hardly get the words out. He kept it to three simple sentences:

"This isn't a real movie, at least not yet. It's only a trailer. But all seven of us worked really hard on it, and we hope you like it."

Then he did a little bow, because he didn't know what else to do, and scurried back to his seat. Thankfully, Izzy and Godfrey were on top of things, lowering the lights and starting the projector back up. It had all been leading to this moment.

The screen was black, music started to play, the crowd quieted, and then . . .

Chapter 37

Carly Lee and the Land of Shadows

Brewster didn't watch the trailer for *Carly Lee and the Land of Shadows*. He'd already seen it hundreds of times. Instead, he watched the people watch the trailer. The people who watched the trailer did the following things:

* They cheered each time a different actor or character showed up on-screen, from Carly, to Palivar, to the Sprite, to the accidental appearance of Liam hiding behind a tree in the background of a shot that Brewster was hoping no one would notice. They noticed.

* They ooohed and aaahed at the special effects. From the lava and the smoke to the ashes and the goo. The Land of Shadows might not have looked like

something from a Hollywood blockbuster, but it certainly didn't look like the real world. It was weird and unique. It was its own thing. Kudos to Harriet.

* They tapped their toes to the beat of the trailer's music, which Brewster had found on a website for songs that were "royalty-free." No one had probably heard the song before, but it worked. It was sufficiently dark and brooding, but also melodic. Plus, it didn't cost anything. Brewster had wanted to use stuff he sometimes heard Jade listening to— songs from bands with curious names like Sigur Rós and Mogwai—but he knew that you had to get permission from the songwriters and performers or, alternatively, pay a boatload of money. Otherwise, the video would be taken down from YouTube for copyright infringement. Royalty-free was the only way to go.

* They whispered to each other, saying things like, "Is that the playground?" and "Wait, how'd they film this at school?" and "I think I know how they did that." Their comments didn't mean they weren't immersed in the trailer. Quite the opposite. It meant they appreciated the work that went into it.

* They pulled their kids or siblings in close, to show them that they were proud of them. This included Brewster's mom, who kissed him on the forehead and patted his knee. "Incredible," she said. Since she wasn't typically an affectionate person, it made the moment both awkward and special. Brewster hoped that he'd remember the special more than the awkward.

* Most of all, they laughed. They laughed at the parts that were supposed to be funny, and the parts that weren't. They laughed at nearly every line of dialogue and at every monster. They laughed at the action sequences that Carly had worked so hard to perfect. They laughed from front to back, all the way up until the final shot of the Snidious Nurk exploding into a splatter of goo and the words *Coming Soon to a Barn Near You!* shooting onto the screen.

* Oh . . . and they clapped. Absolutely thunderous applause. In fact, they gave it a standing ovation.

Chapter 38

A Billion Views

It was a special moment, one that could only be truly appreciated by the people in attendance. Afterward, the guests mingled, and congratulated, and hugged, and had a lovely time. Brewster stumbled through it all in a daze, saying "thank you" over and over again. As a special treat, most of the guests helped clean up before they left, and what might've taken an hour or two was done in minutes. Before long, the filmmakers were the only ones who remained.

Brewster, Carly, Rosa, Godfrey, Izzy, Harriet, and Liam. The lucky seven. They all sat together in a half circle, in the chairs marked with their names, looking up at the movie screen and a projection of Brewster's laptop with YouTube pulled up. The premiere was over, but there was one final thing left to do.

"How long does it take for it to show up online?" Carly asked.

"I've never done one this big," Brewster said as he tapped the keyboard to prepare the video for uploading. "But for the high-def, 4K version, it might take ten to fifteen minutes. I don't know. Maybe even an hour."

"We're willing to wait," Rosa said.

The others agreed. It wasn't hard for them to wait either. They passed the time by joking and reminiscing about the shoot. They complimented each other on their favorite moments from the trailer. They even discussed how they would pay back Piper and Rosa's parents with the money they made once they sold the movie rights to Hollywood.

"How much do you think we'll get?" Harriet asked.

"As long as it covers the amount we owe, I'll be happy," Brewster said.

"Plus interest," Rosa said.

"Plus interest," Brewster echoed.

"That's all the money you want?" Godfrey asked Brewster. "Really and truly?"

Brewster nodded. Really and truly.

"Oh right," Carly said. "All he cares about is if the trailer has a million views."

In all honesty, since waking from his dream that morning, Brewster hadn't thought about the number once. Not a single time. Which had to be a record. And it made him wonder how much he truly cared about it. He cared about it a lot less than he cared about the feeling he was currently having. That was certain. They were together. They were getting along. They were celebrating something they had all created. The premiere had been nice, but overwhelming. This, on the other hand, felt natural. And entirely wonderful. *Forget a million views*, Brewster thought. He didn't want this moment to end.

"You know what's cooler than a million views?" Liam said to everyone.

"What?" they all responded.

"A billion views!" he shouted.

They stared at him.

"It's from a movie," he said, hanging his head. "I'm sorry. I'll stop watching so many movies."

Brewster laughed. He wasn't quite sure why he found it so funny, but he did. And Liam didn't seem to mind. He put up his hands in a gesture that meant *oh well, whatya gonna do?*

"Did you notice something at the premiere?" Rosa asked.

"What?" Brewster said.

"Everybody laughed at everything they saw," Rosa said. "Even the serious stuff."

Brewster had noticed that. And he wasn't sure how he felt about it.

Izzy put it in a good light. "Laughing means they're having fun, right? We wanted them to have fun."

True. But Brewster also wanted them to shriek and gasp

and cry. He wanted the trailer to evoke every possible emotion. Perhaps that was too much to expect.

"Do we have any bloopers we can watch?" Godfrey asked. "That would certainly make *me* laugh."

"What are bloopies?" Harriet asked.

"Bloopers," Izzy told her. "He means funny outtakes that didn't make it into the trailer. They're sometimes shown over the end credits of movies."

"I mean, I guess we have some," Brewster said. "But nothing edited together."

"We have that one," Harriet reminded him. "You know, where Carly fell down?"

"Oh my god!" Carly yelped. "I remember! Yes! Let's watch that!"

It took Brewster a few moments to remember which clip it was, but when he did, it was easy enough to locate on his laptop. And since the trailer was still uploading to YouTube, they had time to watch it. So Brewster projected it on-screen. It was take 5 from the Jumping in the Hole scene, or at least that's how it was logged on Izzy's clapper board, and the clapper board was never wrong.

The moment was undeniably funny, especially since Carly flexed her muscles and snarled at the beginning of the take, before getting a leg tangled in a microphone cord and falling into the Radio Flyer wagon, rolling into the hole, and taking out the green screen, the camera, and the tripod all at once. It was the perfect example of hubris (aka too much self-confidence), but Carly was a good sport. Watching it, she laughed louder than anyone, to the point that there were tears running down her face.

"I bet if we posted that on my TikTok, it'd get those billion views," Carly said, wiping her eyes.

"Yeah, but then it wouldn't be ours anymore," Brewster said. "I kinda want these moments to be between us, and us only. You know what I mean?"

There were no objections. In fact, the others smiled and nodded in agreement. And if he hadn't known it before, Brewster knew then that making the trailer was as important to the other kids as it was to him. In some ways, maybe even more so.

What about the people at the premiere, though? Was it important to them too? Sure, they had laughed and enjoyed themselves, but they were already moving on. No one would ever care about this as much as those seven people in that barn did. Which wasn't a bad thing. It was a great thing, actually, because sharing something like that was an invaluable bond. However, it did mean that Brewster had to be honest. With himself and with his friends.

"In case you don't know, there's a good chance that the trailer won't get a million views," he said.

Harriet wagged a finger. "I don't believe that. I think if—"

"It's true," Brewster said, cutting her off. "I've done this enough to know it's not likely. And that's fine. I'm okay with that."

"We can still sell the rights to the movie for big bucks, though," Carly said.

"Only if we're really lucky," Brewster said. "Like, *really* lucky. Win-the-lottery levels of lucky."

"Why are you talking like this?" Rosa asked.

"Yeah," Izzy said. "We have to make that money back for Piper and Rosa."

"Hear me out," Brewster said. "We already have the camera and the green screens and so many other things. The money might be gone, but we still have each other."

"Meaning?" Rosa asked.

"Meaning . . ." Brewster paused for a moment to collect his thoughts, and then he stood, because directors are supposed to stand when they give speeches. "Meaning that even without a single view on YouTube, we have to keep going. Why should we stop now when we've gotten so much better at this? Remember how clueless we were when we all started? The reason we got better wasn't money. It was because of each other. We can find another way to make the money back. Maybe we'll shoot commercials for businesses in town. You know, videos for their social media accounts? I'd even be open to using Snapchat or TikTok or whatever the latest thing is. It doesn't matter, as long as we keep going. This is worthwhile. *We* are worthwhile. And together, well, we can do so, so much more."

This seemed to perk everyone up, and they each stood as they responded.

"You know I'm game," Liam said.

"And you can always count me in," Harriet added.

"What if we made another trailer?" Izzy proposed.

"Or something even bigger," Godfrey suggested.

"You didn't cover up that hole, did you?" Carly asked.

"No," Brewster responded with a smile because he could see where this was going.

"Our trailer was three minutes long," Rosa said. "How long is a full-length movie?"

"Well," Godfrey replied, "the extended edition of *The Lord of the Rings: The Return of the King* was over four hours and—"

"One hour and fifty-two minutes," Izzy remarked without even consulting her phone "Give or take a few seconds. That's the average."

"And we already have *at least* three minutes filmed," Rosa told them. "We're more than one fortieth of the way there!"

"Is everyone thinking what I'm thinking?" Carly said.

"What are we thinking?" Liam asked.

There was a cardboard box in the corner of the barn holding some green screens, the clapper board, and some of the props and costumes the Tarkingtons hadn't taken home yet. Brewster paced over and hefted it up into his arms.

"I'm thinking it's gonna be the golden hour soon," he said, carrying the box toward the open barn doors. "And we could sit here waiting for this video to finish uploading. Or . . ."

"Oh, I get it," Liam said with a grin.

"What are we waiting for, then?" Rosa asked.

Nothing, presumably. Because with determined looks on their faces, they all started marching toward the exit, ready to get to work. Outside the breeze was strong enough to make the leaves on the maple trees dance and shimmer in the spring light. Brewster was tempted to say the air smelled like potential, but he didn't know if potential had a scent. It smelled nice, in any case. And the mountains and the fields and the clouds and the, well, *everything* seemed just right for an evening of shooting. The golden hour was fast approaching, but they were ready. And that's when Carly remembered something important.

"Oh. We need a script first, don't we?"

Chapter 39

Coming Soon to a Barn Near You . . .

CARLY LEE AND THE LAND OF SHADOWS
The Screenplay for the
Full-Length Feature Film!

A Collaboration Between
Brewster Gaines, Carly Lee, Rosa Blake,
Godfrey Tarkington, Isolde Tarkington,
Harriet Joseph, and Liam Wentworth

A "FIND A WAY" PRODUCTION

Acknowledgments

Novels, like videos and movies, are collaborative efforts, and this particular novel is the result of the dedication and talents of the following people:

Alex Wolfe

Rob Valois

Michael Bourret

Kristen Head

Caroline Press

Shara Hardeson

Ana Deboo

Rima Weinberg

Sophie Erb

Vanessa DeJesús

Chris Danger

And the rest of the team at Penguin Workshop and PRH

Of course, I could not have even dreamt of writing it without the love and support of my family, particularly Cate, Hannah, Rowan, Tom, Randi, Toril, Tim, Jim, Gwenn, Dave, Magela, Pete, Jacob, Will, Matteo, and Mauro.

And finally, I want to thank all those kids from the Brookside neighborhood in Fayetteville, New York. You humored me and sometimes even encouraged me whenever I pointed a camcorder in your face. It made a difference.